MAJOR INVASION AND OTHER STORIES

PETER KENNEDY

Copyright © Peter Kennedy 2023
This book is sold subject to the condition that it shall not, by way of trade or otherwise, be lent, resold, hired out, or otherwise circulated without the publisher's prior consent in any form of binding or cover other than that in which it is published and without a similar condition including this condition being imposed on the subsequent publisher.
The moral right of Peter Kennedy has been asserted.
ISBN-13: 9798379277758

This is a work of fiction. Names, characters, businesses, places, events and incidents are either the products of the author's imagination or used in a fictitious manner. Any resemblance to actual persons, living or dead, or actual events is purely coincidental.

For Catherine, Luke and Vanessa.

CONTENTS

Malignant Invasion *1*
Speak The Word *40*
Now You See It *51*
A Question Of Statistics *66*
Past And Present *75*
No Redemption *86*
Select *96*
The Light *127*
Spider *135*
About The Author *140*

MALIGNANT INVASION

NOAH

I'm called Noah and, regrettably, my primary purpose is to slowly destroy the lives of human beings. It is not my choice to do this, you must understand, but this is just my lot in life, or, to be more accurate, my lot in another being's death. I do have other more familiar names such as motor neuron disease (MND) or, as clever neurologists tend to call me, amyotrophic lateral sclerosis (ALS), and also Lou Gehrig's Disease, an eponymous label that I have always found rather too personal despite its popularity in the United States. Anyway, I have never liked baseball.

To be perfectly honest with you, I am still not absolutely sure why I came into being in the first place, though I know for sure that I do exist. That is very much the case as I'm certain everyone would agree, especially those poor unfortunate souls who are the victims of my all-encompassing and highly malignant presence. I suppose it all boils down to a natural balance of life and death, with every event in human existence necessarily having an equal and opposite force that helps keep it under control and which maintains everyone in a low but constant state of fear. There really is no doubt about it – I have an extremely bad reputation. In fact, I am hated and feared in equal measure by afflicted patients, their relatives and of course their doctors. Neurologists really loathe my guts. Everyone who uses his or her brain fears me for what I might do to them – cruelly curtail what may well have been a happy and productive life. But you must understand that I have never had any real choice in the matter. I am just doing what I have been instructed to do by whatever or whoever created me in the first place. I may be seen to act in a vicious manner but, and you must believe me, I have nothing against the human race personally. Actually, I have always rather admired human beings. I do the terrible things I do because I am programmed that way by a higher entity or force, the nature and identity of which I do not know and probably never will. When it comes to understanding what controls us all in both health and disease I am as much in the dark as my victims. I prefer this latter term because it is clearly more accurate and less euphemistic than calling them my subjects or hosts. I know full well what I am and the mental and physical havoc that I inevitably wreak on human beings. Such is my fate. Such is my purpose. It's regrettable to be sure, but absolutely true.

*

For the sake of openness I think I ought to explain my *raison-d'etre*, so to speak, in just a little detail. What I cause is known by human experts in the field as a neurodegenerative disease and, I must admit, an extremely nasty and usually rapidly progressive one at that. I know for certain that one or two of my disease-causing brethren can also cause progressive maladies of the human nervous system, but I reckon I'm far worse than all of them put together. I am not proud of that at all – in fact, I actually regret it. But I guess that's just life, or to be more accurate, death.

The mechanism of this destruction is surprisingly explicable, though it will be a very long time, if ever, before the true underlying cause of my existence and actions are discovered by humans. Frankly they are all barking up the wrong tree and I reckon that won't change in the foreseeable future. I cause a progressive and relentless destruction of the nerve cells (or neurons to be specific) in the brain and spinal cord. This causes a pretty stereotypical pattern of symptoms and signs, and I never cease to be amazed at how quick and perceptive most of the specialist neurologists are at diagnosing my handiwork. Victims become progressively weaker and eventually lose the power in their arms and legs, often starting in just one muscle or group of muscles in the arms or hands. Eventually the stricken (or, more accurately, the randomly chosen) sufferers develop terrible difficulties with chewing, swallowing and speaking; their emotions sometimes become totally inappropriate, even for humans; they get frightening breathing difficulties so that some even get put onto an artificial ventilator, which prolongs their life but doesn't stop the degeneration; and they finally die about two to four years after diagnosis from aspiration pneumonia. Not very nice I'm sure you will agree. No wonder everyone fears me, especially the men whom I attack rather more frequently than women. Well, after all, I do still have a certain modicum of gallantry as you must no doubt concede. But some doctors think I'm the worst disease that anyone can get and, I have to admit, they may well have a point though actually I think there are still a few conditions even worse than me, though not all of them are caused by a disease entity, but more a question of bad luck like a young man becoming tetraplegic after a motor accident or unwisely diving into an empty swimming pool. Ouch!

But I am not totally without compassion, difficult as that may be to believe. Though involved a bit in the degeneration, I don't destroy Onuf's nucleus in the front of the lower spinal cord so my victims are still able to use their sphincters normally and sexual function is not affected. And I don't stray out of my territory so the nerves which control sensation are not affected. I am a motor person through and through. I think that's quite enough damage, don't you?

JAMES

As he sat comfortably by his office computer quietly consuming his frugal lunch – more like a midday snack than a proper meal – Dr James Purloyne couldn't help thinking about his tally of neurological outpatients that day, six anxious souls in all. It was a pretty typical morning's work, with most of the patients suffering from little more than anxiety about the possibility of serious illness. In reality, most of them could be regarded as the 'worried well' and he did his best to reassure them, something that he's always been particularly good at. James is as kind as he is medically astute. But one of his referrals concerned him greatly. The patient in question was a very pleasant man, aged sixty-three, though he looked much older, and still nearly a decade more than James who certainly hopes he'll look better than that when he enters his sixties. His name was Mr Jordan Smith, and James, who has gained a reputation as an excellent diagnostician, strongly suspects that this unfortunate individual has the early symptoms and signs of something very bad. This view owes as much to instinct as to medical knowledge and, of course, he could be completely wrong about everything, but he knows in his heart that such a thing is unlikely. Even as a very young trainee doctor, James had an irritating propensity for getting things right about patients, something that annoyed as many colleagues as it delighted. While his detractors were usually fellow doctors or those half-way up the slippery hierarchy, his admirers were invariably his senior colleagues and consultant bosses who were already at the top of their game.

After quickly consuming what just about passes for lunch, including a rather poor excuse for an espresso coffee, he spent the next thirty minutes dictating letters about the people he'd seen that morning. What really worried him about the one potentially sick patient was the unusual pattern of right-hand weakness that didn't seem to conform to any definite nerve root or pathological process. A greatly respected and now dead boss of his from a decade before had once told him that whenever a patient presented in this strange, almost indefinable, way, then one must always entertain a diagnosis of very early motor neuron disease, or MND for short. If that proved to be the case, it would certainly be very bad news for Mr Smith and, in his long experience, even more catastrophic for his family. Anyway, James quickly arranged an urgent hospital admission for the man. Both fingers and toes were firmly crossed.

*

James spent the rest of that Tuesday doing a variety of jobs that he had somehow avoided for many days. There was always more paperwork to do. He was aware that he was basically killing time in what was, essentially, the human equivalent of animal displacement activities, but he had to earn his relatively high salary somehow. While that may seem like a rather jaundiced or cynical view to an outsider, the sad fact is that this self-perception seemed more than real to him, such was his innate modesty or lack of self-esteem, both of which found expression at different times of his life and in a welter of varied circumstances. A lot of medical doctors probably suffer from that particular form of delusion. But the real problem for the profession is that some doctors, especially surgeons, certainly do not, and raise an overbearing persona to what could be best described as an art form.

He ended the day thinking intensely about Jordan Smith. Though he had a pretty good working knowledge of the human nervous system, in both health and disease, James was very much an instinctive physician, one who was influenced as much by what his gut told him as by his medical knowledge. As such, this made him an unusual doctor, but he seldom talked about his slightly eccentric method of reaching a diagnosis to his colleagues, even to the small number he regarded as close to him. After all, everyone has a limit as to what they might believe, and he had no wish to stand out as an eccentric individual. Once labelled as such, few doctors ever manage to shake off the hackles that accompany a label of eccentricity, one which would forever deprive him of the trust of most of his professional colleagues, even the ones he considered friends. Be that as it may, he had a distinct and very clear notion that his patient would turn out to have motor neuron disease. Perhaps a premonition would be a better description. His instincts could sometimes be a real pain, but he just couldn't avoid them.

There was something about computer gazing and paperwork that in some mysterious way caused a rapid passing of time, a strange but also reassuring phenomenon that was as consistent as it was also surprising. Before he was even aware of it, James noticed that the large round wall clock in his small office already showed 5.50 in the late afternoon, a perfectly acceptable time of the day for him to shut up shop and leave for home. Feeling just a little guilty for some irrational reason, he did just that and within five minutes he found himself in the driver's seat of his comfortable Audi automatic in the hospital's sprawling underground car park.

It took just twenty minutes for James to drive to his elegant house in Highgate, a prosperous region of

London, and not very far from his London teaching hospital base. Everything in his car seemed as it should though he was slightly surprised that the temperature gauge on his neat driver's console showed an unexpectedly high reading. While it didn't seem to affect the movement of the car, nevertheless he couldn't ignore it and made a mental note to check the water level in the front radiator later that evening after the car had cooled down sufficiently to avoid his getting scalded. James was no mechanic for sure but he did have a layman's rudimentary knowledge of the basic workings of an automobile.

For some reason he was more than usually happy to be greeted on arrival by Veronica, his wife of thirty years, and his two teenage children, Paul and Clare, who were just two years apart in age. After a brief visit to the bathroom both to relieve himself and to wash his hands like the surgeon that he never was, they all sat down to a typically sumptuous dinner in the house's small but cosy dining room. Whoever said that the way to a man's heart is through his stomach was obviously joking, but nevertheless that person may well have had a point. Every mouthful of delicious seafood was a particularly high form of gustatory pleasure. The large scallops were perhaps a little chewy but they were still delicious to be sure, and he had no problem devouring them.

Soon after they had eaten, James remembered the

promise he'd made to himself about checking the water in the car; he had to act quickly since it was early October and it would soon be so dark that it would make a visual inspection well-nigh impossible, especially as the Audi had been parked outside the house and not in the garage which was already housing his wife's smaller Volkswagen. It was already getting cool outside as James deactivated the car's security system using the function attached to his keys, opened the driver's door and then flipped the bonnet opening switch located just below the steering wheel. Running his fingers under the edge of the car bonnet he elevated the whole bonnet structure and fixed it upright and open using an inbuilt meal rod attached to the underside of the bonnet. He quickly located the car radiator and, so far as he could see, the water level seemed pretty normal. But to be sure, he needed to unscrew the metal cap on top of the radiator which also acted as a type of pressure valve. He used his right hand to do this, something that had presented no problem at all in the past, as both his wrist movements were strong, in fact rather stronger than one would imagine from his slender frame. But something was wrong. Try as he might, he just couldn't muster the wrist strength to twist the screw cap open. The power just wasn't there. When he tried again using his left hand, he was able to unscrew the cap easily and view the water level which, to his relief, was indeed quite normal and healthy. Why he should have lost the normal power in his right hand was a complete mystery to him. But he soon dismissed this weakness as being due to tiredness. He wasn't unduly concerned. Which just shows how wrong you can be.

NOAH

Well, there you have it. I have now started the disease process which, all being well for me (but not for James), should take about two years in all from the start to the end, give or take. Normally, I don't do irony, but the more I think about it, the more I see that it is truly ironic that I have attacked James at the same time as one of my disease clones has decided to infiltrate the nervous system of one of his patients. Look, I never said that life (or ultimately death in this case) was either fair or predictable. Quite the opposite is the case.

Of course the unfortunate victim may die rather sooner than two years if he or she succumbs to some unpredictable event like choking on a chicken bone or a piece of steak and ends up contracting a very nasty aspiration pneumonia. That really isn't part of the overall plan despite its obvious finality. But at the opposite end of the spectrum, people really shouldn't live with me for a very long period after the diagnosis. But when they do, I can't help feeling a high degree of regard for them despite my failure to finish them off pretty quickly. Of course I'm thinking of that admirable scientific genius Stephen Hawking who lived for over fifty years after first being diagnosed when he was a brilliant physics student at Oxford. I know he had a bit of help from his friends and medical staff but nevertheless he was a remarkable outlier in terms of his relative and totally unexpected longevity. I did my best, but his will was just too great to be defeated. He had too much science to do, and he also managed to have a family with a wife and three children. So I certainly failed there, though I was soundly beaten by a truly brilliant human, except I suppose in a way one could argue that I somehow got him in the end.

Interestingly, despite the initial random nature of the weakness, as the disease progresses there is invariably a certain order of muscle failure. Order is so important in life don't you think? The last muscles to be affected are those controlling the eyes and cheek movements, and just about everyone will remember how Hawking used to communicate in a most painstaking manner by employing the slightest movements of his cheek to indicate different letters of the alphabet. Then engineering maestros converted those words into a rather weird American voice that people couldn't help associating with the great scientist. As I have said before, I just can't help admiring some human beings, and there seems to be no limit to human ingenuity when battling against the dreadful ravages that I have no option but to produce. Of course, if the victim's breathing can be somehow maintained then inevitable death can be postponed for many years. They are particularly good at doing that in America.

Naturally, during the normal (or, to be more accurate, abnormal) course of events the unfortunate victim has very limited time left, but the disease, myself that is, has all the time in the world. To make it easier for everyone reading this account, confession or whatever you want to call it, I have been referring to myself as a distinct entity. I can be referred to as a 'he' for the sake of simplicity, but in reality, I am neither a 'he' nor a 'she' but, if you will, just a highly malignant 'it'. Whoever said that one should always 'know thyself' was certainly talking great sense. I know exactly what I am, what I am capable of, and what I intend to do.

JAMES

James was no fool, but his main problems were fear and denial. He was fearful about what his hand weakness may portend and, like many medical doctors, he was apt to deny the faintest possibility that he may have a serious disease, and a neurological one at that. Besides, like many doctors, James was an inveterate hypochondriac which only made things worse.

The following morning he performed a minor experiment on himself, though no-one observing him – not even Veronica, his kind and compassionate wife – would have had the remotest idea that this was what he was doing. For Veronica and his two teenage children, it was just an ordinary breakfast with everyone eating and drinking as they had always done for years. In James's case, his high fibre cereal was followed by brown toast and jam. The old jam jar being empty, his immediate task was to open a new one which required a fair degree of wrist strength, a twisting movement that had never defeated him in the past. But it would require about the same degree of pressure to open the jar as had been required the previous evening when he had tried unsuccessfully to open the car radiator cap. Naturally, he failed to twist the lid open. His failure was observed by Paul, at seventeen years the slightly older of his two children, who gave his father a quizzical look and then proceeded to open the jam jar with relative ease.

'I must have strained my wrist yesterday while trying to fix the car,' James explained.

'Sure Dad,' his son replied.

But while his family was not concerned in the

least, James was starting to become a little more worried than he had been the night before. He couldn't help feeling that something sinister was going on, however much he might try to deny it and think of a whole range of alternative and benign causes for his newfound weakness. The key problem was that he had always rather prided himself on the strength of his wrists and hands which seemed to be belied by his slender frame. So even the slightest of changes was immediately noticed. And fear invariably trumps pride.

*

Later that morning, James drove into the hospital's sprawling underground car park, took the tiny claustrophobic lift and made his way briskly to his modest office in the modern outpatients department. He believed in getting the bulk of his routine clinical work almost completely finished by the middle of the week so he had another clinic to carry out that day, though this time it was primarily for return patients, plus any special referrals, usually from colleagues' relatives who were mostly the 'worried well'. After all, he did have a reputation for thoroughness and a high level of quiet competence. It occurred to James that while examining some of his patients he might also be able to surreptitiously get an idea of his own arm and hand power. The very idea rather went against his natural professional inclinations but he felt that he really had no choice in the matter. As the old saying goes – 'needs must'.

Half-way through the clinic of twelve souls, he realised that he'd so far not had an opportunity to try out his slightly unethical plan, one that involved a reversal of the normal patient–doctor dynamic. But the seventh case was just right. This was an otherwise fit middle-aged man who had presented with what James thought was a mainly 'functional' or non-organic set of symptoms which didn't unduly worry him, though they caused a great deal of worry in the patient himself. He decided to give the man a cursory physical examination, in part to reassure the poor man that nothing serious was going on, but also to test his own strength. When it came to limb power, James tested each arm muscle of the patient in his usual careful manner, but in assessing the man's wrist power, in particular wrist flexion and extension, James was also able to surreptitiously assess the strength of his own right wrist. The result was unequivocal. He was definitely weaker than his patient, meaning his underlying fear about what was happening to his own body was both justified and real. Something was clearly amiss but exactly what was wrong still eluded him. At this stage he preferred to continue in a state of denial in the forlorn hope that the irksome problem would just go away by itself. Pigs might fly.

NOAH

I strongly suspect James has a very good idea as to what is the matter with him, but he just doesn't dare to admit to himself what he knows is the most likely diagnosis. Every time I strike, it's the same old story. Those people who know nothing about medicine have no idea what's wrong until their neurologist gives them the definitive diagnosis. And the very people who have all the necessary medical knowledge to work it out for themselves just look the other way. It has probably always been like this since the beginning of human civilisation. It really is a wonder to me and my kind just how many people suffering from my particular affliction remain in a complete state of denial, and I have come to the conclusion that physicians are the worst offenders in this regard. They are also, of course, such dreadful hypochondriacs even when they contract something really serious that will almost certainly end their health and, most probably, terminate their existence.

Now it's only been about two months since I started the whole unfortunate business, and very soon I shall give James something to really worry about. I think it's just about the right time to increase the pace of my disease, my unstoppable infiltration of his fragile nervous system. You know, I almost feel sorry for him, but such feelings would be totally unprofessional and must be disregarded and consigned to the gutter of impossible empathy. My word, I am starting to sound like one of my victims, and that would never do.

JAMES

It had been four months since the first symptom developed and, understandably, James had been getting increasingly concerned about his health. He was now convinced, astute diagnostician that he is despite his innate hypochondriasis, that he was suffering from a serious and progressive neurological disease. All of the evidence was there and just plain to see. The time and opportunity for denial had long since passed.

The key moment for him, the one that changed his entire mindset, had occurred just a month previously. He had experienced a hard day at the hospital, having seen six new outpatients, all of them difficult cases, as well as two personal referrals, even trickier inpatients under the care of two of his colleagues who greatly valued his medical opinion. When he eventually arrived at his home in Highgate the first thing he did was rush for the shower, even though he was by that time ravenously hungry after the day's exertions and his meagre lunchtime snack. As the refreshing hot water from the overhead nozzle irrigated and soothed his weary body, he couldn't fail to notice some slight, but definite, twitching of the small muscles of his right hand which also looked slightly wasted to his experienced eye. This was in addition to the right wrist weakness that had become slightly, but relentlessly, worse over the previous three months but which he had chosen to ignore completely despite the worry it caused. He also couldn't fail to notice some slight but definite twitching of the muscles in his left calf, despite the absence of weakness in either of his legs. It was at this point that James realised that he might well have the dreaded motor neuron disease. But he needed to know for sure and more evidence of such a malady was required.

The following day was a much easier one for James in terms of workload and things he had to do. Never one to procrastinate in life and put off until tomorrow what he might do today, nevertheless he was also a pragmatist and had a keen sense of priorities. There seemed little point in carrying on with his benevolent work for afflicted patients when he himself might well be harbouring some awful disease. No, that just would not do. He must prioritise his own good health. It wasn't selfish but just good common sense.

Around mid-morning, in between dictating the never-ending stream of letters on his hand-held Dictaphone, James found the courage to take the difficult but necessary step of phoning one of his most trusted and gifted colleagues. The doctor in question was none other than Dr John Rapello, a thirty-eight-year-old consultant neurologist of huge ability but also with an unusual talent that was tinged with a distinctly human flavour so that the resulting mix was one of combined competence and kindness. He was also a very jovial character of Italian extraction which somehow made him a most agreeable person to have as a professional colleague. John was also extremely discreet. That was a quality that James particularly admired.

Within two hours of their phone call, James was knocking gently on the door of John's spacious and tidy office which contained a small examination couch just beside the large window at the front. He nervously greeted his younger colleague. The two men shook hands warmly and James was politely asked to sit down in one of the three upholstered chairs that were located close to the neurologist's oblong desk. James noted the framed photograph of John's wife and two young children that had been placed at an angle on the left side of the desk, a reassuring reminder that he was about to spout out all his symptoms and fears to a man who was clearly going to understand the predicament that he was about to describe.

'Right then,' said John, 'let's have it from the beginning.'

'I will tell you everything that's happened to me

over the last three months or so, I promise, and I shan't leave anything out. I will be just like any other patient.'

'Good,' replied John, 'that's very good – actually, it's the only way. You know that James.'

'Yes I do for sure,' answered James.

Over the next ten minutes, James gave a remarkably clear and concise chronological account of his symptoms, during which time he was not interrupted even once. His doctor certainly knew how and when to listen to a patient, eminent or otherwise.

When James had finished, John looked distinctly worried but still managed to strike a lighter note. 'So I presume there's been no tennis for the last few months?'

'Spot on John, none whatsoever.'

John then asked several probing questions, all of them designed to get further clarification of the story, something that he had always been very good at. He was particularly keen to know whether there had been any problems with speech or swallowing and whether there was any family history of a neurological illness. Following this medical cross-examination he proceeded with the physical examination of his patient. This was carried out with his usual speed and precision during which he never changed his stony-faced expression. Indeed he remained completely inscrutable.

After another ten minutes of careful scrutiny of his colleague's nervous system John had completed his assessment.

'So what do you think?' asked James.

'Well it's not completely straightforward,' was the immediate reply.

'Really?' asked James. 'You don't think I've got MND?'

John smiled and looked James straight in the eyes. 'Sure, MND is a real possibility but the diagnosis is certainly not definite and it could still be something else…'

'Like what do you think?'

'Well,' John continued, 'for a start, while you do have some wasting and fasciculation…'

'You mean twitching when you say that?'

'Yes indeed… As I was saying, you do have some suggestive signs in your right hand and wrist but you don't have evidence of combined upper and lower motor neuron signs in the same muscle group which you really need to make a definite diagnosis of MND.'

'That's good I suppose,' said James, 'unless, I guess, it's a form of progressive muscular atrophy with only wasting and weakness and no upper motor neuron signs.'

'Yes, that's right. Also we need to exclude

something going on in your neck. You mentioned that you've been getting a lot of neck pain in recent months. You know that cervical spondylosis can mimic a range of conditions including MND.'

'Yes of course... So I guess you'll arrange an electromyogram to look at the electrical activity in my muscles and an MRI scan of my cervical spine to work it all out?'

'Yes, right first time. I'll get these organised, plus a few routine blood tests, as soon as possible. Anyway, you're one of us and I'm sure I can pull a few strings to get these tests scheduled within a week or two.'

'Thank you, John. I really appreciate it.'

'A pleasure... Let's keep our fingers and toes firmly crossed.'

*

Five days later, James found himself sitting quietly but nervously in the small waiting room of the hospital's highly regarded Clinical Neurophysiology department. How many times had he, as a consultant neurologist, referred his patients to these clever doctors? Yet now he was there as an anxious patient and not as a doctor so he had to completely change his mindset. That was a much easier thing for him to do than he might have thought, almost like a kind of reversion to childhood and the need to be looked after. Within just a few minutes, he, the eminent Dr James Purloyne, found himself courteously beckoned into the examination room by a senior nurse where he was greeted warmly by Dr Wolf Levitsky, another of his colleagues, a clinical neurophysiologist of considerable experience and ability. He hopped onto the examination couch and let Wolf get on with the job in hand, a procedure that must have been as routine for the electrophysiologist as it was terrifying for James who had little difficulty playing the role of a patient.

The entire examination took little more than twenty minutes. First, cool metal electrodes were placed on the surface of the muscles of his hands, arms and legs, then needles were placed into the muscles of his hands which hurt him a great deal, and finally the conduction velocities of his motor and sensory nerves were carefully measured. Throughout the procedure Wolf remained completely inscrutable, professional doctor that he was. But he had already realised what the unfortunate diagnosis was before he smiled at James, telling him that he would be in touch in a day or two, after he had studied the results carefully.

'But don't you know already from the initial tests?' James asked nervously.

'No, I need to work out all the velocities and look at the electrical traces, especially the results from the surface electrodes. It won't take me very long and of course I'll treat this as an absolute priority.'

'OK, fair enough,' replied James, not entirely convinced.

'Just give me some time and I'll give you my best assessment, and I'll also speak with John Rapello. He was very keen to get all this sorted out as soon as possible.'

'Fine, thank you. I really appreciate it, and for doing this so quickly.'

With that, James walked out of the investigation suite and awaited his fate.

Of course, both John Rapello and Wolf Levitsky were already pretty sure which neurological disease had afflicted their esteemed colleague. The MRI scan of his cervical spine had only showed minor degenerative changes. They were convinced that the bad news needed to be broken to James as gently as possible. Fat chance of that.

NOAH

Poor James has just been told by his doctor that he has full-blown MND and will be lucky to survive even two years. Well, it will be even shorter than that if I have anything to do with it. It will be, I hope, more like one year or perhaps one and a half years if his doctors are up to scratch. From what I have seen so far, I am sure they are just that. I must admit that

James has been pretty brave throughout the whole sorry diagnostic business; it is his long-suffering wife Veronica who has taken it particularly badly. That is not an uncommon observation. After all, James is fifty-five years old and they have been married for thirty years – it's hardly surprising that she doesn't want to lose her life partner with whom she has been particularly close. I note that he hasn't yet told his two teenage children, Paul and Clare, about the dreadful diagnosis, but in due course he will have to do that. In my long experience, complete openness is usually best in these situations, and he can't just run away from the diagnosis and pretend it isn't happening. Sooner rather than later is the best thing to do.

My word, just see how much terrible suffering I have caused this family who until recently had known neither real fear nor severe illness. You know, I almost feel sorry for them, but that would be unprofessional and, besides, I have a job to do, however awful the consequences. Business is business as they say.

I am also aware that James has just had a choking fit, which I am sure will be the first of many such episodes. That will surely be the case if I am doing my job properly. Sometimes I come close to hating myself almost as much as I hate my victims.

JAMES

It was now just over six months since the onset of his symptoms. When James was told several weeks before of the terrible diagnosis of MND, he was still shocked by the raw reality of the situation even though he had expected this news for some time. After all, he was no fool and indeed was an astute diagnostician though doctors are just like the rest of humanity in terms of denying what is so obvious to just about everyone else. Not only did he have typical symptoms of the disease, but the electromyogram was clearly diagnostic and there really was no other possibility. The unfortunate diagnosis was unequivocal. His wife was even more upset than her husband about his illness, something that is not uncommon in situations like these. While both of them knew full well what the diagnosis would mean in terms of future disability and long-term prognosis, it was she who for some reason had a more vivid and fearful picture of what the immediate future held for both of them as well as their two children. Neither of the children truly understood the full implications of the diagnosis, but both of them could not help noticing the appalling change in their parents' general demeanour, and they may well have had more insight into the serious situation than James and Veronica suspected, at least initially. Never underestimate the quiet insights and robustness of the younger generation. To do so is invariably a great mistake.

*

James had always been a practical man, a quality generally required for people in his profession. With his new diagnosis at the forefront of his mind, he was keen to do and achieve everything possible over the one year that he probably had left before his inevitable physical decline. He therefore decided, very sensibly, to take early retirement on health grounds. To arrange this, he needed to explain exactly why to the hospital's general manager, a sympathetic, intensely pragmatic and intelligent woman called Janet Grangeholm, a person who until two years before her hospital appointment was a senior executive in a highly successful supermarket chain. How times change, James thought to himself.

As James slowly and carefully entered Janet's large and plush office, moving rather tentatively as his walking and balance were already mildly compromised by his illness, she immediately arose from her blue upholstered chair and greeted him more warmly than he had been used to.

'James,' she said to him directly, 'it's good to see you again.'

'It's good to see you too Janet,' was his polite reply.

She began to look a little uneasy, if not slightly embarrassed, as she beckoned James to sit down and feel at ease. 'I've heard about your diagnosis James, and I want to say just how sorry I am.'

'Thanks Janet. I guess it's just one of those things… Life is a lottery and my run of good luck just stopped. It's an awful situation I'm in but there's absolutely nothing I can do about it.'

Janet eased up slightly and decided to engage him a little in conversation. 'How is your family coping with the news?'

'Well,' James started before hesitating. 'Veronica used to be a nurse so she knows the score. At first, she was shocked and terrified, just as I was, but recently she seems to have kind of come to terms with the diagnosis. As for the children, I'm really not completely sure, but I suspect they don't really appreciate what the future holds for me.'

'The future is pretty grim then I guess,' Janet added.

'Yes, good choice of words. I suspect I'll last about another year or so, maybe eighteen months…'

'Oh goodness…'

'Of course that's assuming I actually want to last the course, what with all the physical suffering and humiliation that it's clearly going to involve.'

'What do you mean James?'

'I'm referring to Dignitas in Switzerland of course where euthanasia is legal. I may want to terminate my life prematurely rather than suffer the ravages of the disease… It's only a thought of course.'

'A pretty frightening one at that but I would certainly understand if you decided to go down that path.'

'Thanks Janet but I don't have to decide anything like that right now.'

'Of course not.'

There followed a tangibly awkward silence of perhaps twenty seconds at the most, though at the time it seemed much longer to them both. Time is always a relative dimension.

James was the first to break the silence. 'Janet, I'm sure you can understand that for a whole variety of reasons I'm very keen to take early retirement on health grounds.'

Janet wasn't even remotely surprised or fazed by this request which actually came as a relief to her rather than a demand from a difficult physician. After all, James had mentioned the issue first so that relieved her of the burden of broaching it with him.

She smiled sympathetically rather than sweetly, in tune with the gravity of their discussion, and spoke briefly but directly. 'James, I think early retirement due to your MND is entirely reasonable and I fully support it. I also find it inconceivable that anyone in the Health

Board would raise the slightest objection. Far from it, and I've no doubt that everyone in the hospital and management system would have enormous sympathy for you and understanding. Consider it done.'

'Well, it's good to know that doctors and managers can completely agree on something, even if it does take a uniformly fatal neurological disease to achieve such a result.'

Janet smiled and just said, 'Well put, James. Sad but well put anyway.'

*

Janet was as good as her word and James was very soon granted early retirement from his prestigious, though physically and mentally demanding, consultant medical position in the hospital on health grounds. He was both moved and surprised by the many sympathetic and clearly heartfelt messages he received from several of his regular patients, most of whom were deeply saddened at his illness but also very disheartened at the prospect of losing such a kind, caring and competent doctor.

His main concern at that time was to decide how best to use the limited time that he had left – perhaps just a few months of relative mobility and reasonable health followed by a rapid decline in many of his key neurological functions. The very thought terrified both him and his wife. Above all, they wanted to travel to places they had never visited, but they had not considered the thorny issue of travel insurance for one so ill, not to mention the possibility of an acute exacerbation of his condition while away on vacation. For these very cogent reasons, they decided to limit their travel plans to the United Kingdom, in particular Scotland which they had scarcely explored despite the great physical beauty of Perthshire and the Highland regions.

While they managed to take a few brief trips to both England and Scotland, usually with Veronica doing most of the driving, things took a distinct turn for the worse just six months after the initial diagnosis. At first, he would only choke on his food occasionally, but these terrifying and hugely distressing choking episodes became more frequent, especially when he tried to swallow tough meat which therefore disappeared from his wife's menu. At this stage, he was perfectly able to swallow liquids. But he had also noticed the beginning of other failures of his body's normal functioning. Though it was still slight, and hardly noticeable by others, James began to be aware of a distinct difficulty with his speech. He knew exactly what he wanted to say, but sometimes words came out slurred and sentences indistinct compared to his usual clear, well-articulated and precise manner of speaking. It was significant that Veronica had also noticed this difficulty though she said nothing to him about it. But she was all too aware of the downhill direction in which James was travelling. She was a highly intelligent and knowledgeable woman with a good grasp of medicine, though clearly not as much as her husband who remained relatively stoical, at least at this relatively early stage of the disease.

Soon after his speech and swallowing difficulties James became aware of an increasing unsteadiness while walking, which he realised was due to a weakness in his legs and back, and the muscles in his hands became increasingly wasted, the right more than the left. While never an obese person – indeed quite the opposite, he had always been pretty slim – he also became aware of a slow and insidious weight loss which could not be completely explained by his eating less food. But otherwise he felt reasonably normal in that his sensation was entirely normal everywhere, he was quite able to pass water normally and, remarkably, if not ironically in view of their mental state, he and Veronica were still able to make love though, increasingly, she had to take the lead, so to speak, because of his increasing weakness.

NOAH

Well, it's now been exactly one year since my most unfortunate victim first became aware that something was going severely wrong in his body, or to be more specific, in his nervous system. Of course, as I'm sure you all realise, I was invading the hapless James for quite a while before that. His cards, so to speak, had been marked even at that very early pre-symptomatic stage. But clearly James is now in really deep trouble. Wisely, he has long quit his high-powered medical job because, possessing the insight that one would expect from a talented physician like him, he was aware that his progressive neurodegenerative illness would make him far less able to function as a doctor, and also because he dearly wants, if he possibly can, to enjoy the short amount of time he has left to live on the planet. Well, this planet anyway. If only all of my victims showed such good sense. Having said that, quite a few people, especially neurologists, have noticed that I have a distinct tendency to invade nice, agreeable human beings rather than the twenty-four carat bastards who so commonly populate the Earth. This is purely an observation by many, but in reality, it is, I openly admit, quite true. I just find it so much easier to destroy the lives of nice, decent people. Does that make me an evil being? I suspect probably not. But perhaps it is a sad reflection of my fundamentally malign nature. Actually, I still sometimes affect truly nasty people so I do have a sense of balance if you get my meaning. Within the next few months, things are going to get a great deal worse for James. Mark my words, they will. They definitely will. From now on, the gloves are off. As if they were ever on, I hear you say.

JAMES

Things went from bad to worse for James over the next three months. His swallowing of both solids and liquids had deteriorated to such an extent that his doctors suggested to him that the best course of action would be to be fed through a plastic gastrostomy tube inserted surgically through his abdominal wall into his stomach. While, understandably, he was initially reluctant to undergo this surgical procedure, he was eventually persuaded by his wife and doctors that it would be a very good idea. If that were not enough discomfort for anyone, his walking had become almost impossible, necessitating the use of an electric wheelchair which he found particularly humiliating since he had always been a highly independent individual. How he hated the wheelchair.

What about his speech? His ability to communicate coherently to anyone, including his family, had become very difficult as his uttered words were so indistinct. Because of this he was forced to use a small device given to him by his kindly speech therapist into which he would type the words he was trying to speak. The machine would show the digital form of the words that he had typed. He had not, however, managed to acquire the sophisticated voice synthesiser which converted the typed words into the now familiar American voice that the world had always recognised as belonging to the great scientist Stephen Hawking who had a form of MND which he managed to battle for over fifty years. Where there's a will, then for sure there's a way.

The one condition that James really dreaded was pneumonia, as he fully realised that he might well end up on an artificial ventilator which he just didn't want even if it might prolong his life by weeks and months, if not potentially by years. He had already had two episodes of bacterial pneumonia, no doubt due, at least in part, to the weakness of his chest intercostal muscles which are required for breathing normally. These had been treated effectively with antibiotics and intensive physiotherapy. During these times, James had very seriously considered terminating his life prematurely at Dignitas in Switzerland, but he had thought better of that route which he decided to banish from his mind. This was due not only to his desire to keep living however ill he might be, but also out of a fear of the legal implications for his wife who would need to accompany him. Anyway, life is sweet, however bad it is.

NOAH

Well, we are now nearly at the end of the unfortunate process after one and a half years, just as I had initially predicted. Sometimes I marvel at the accuracy of my prognostic predictions. Poor James has been using the dreaded wheelchair for several months because of his limb weakness, he is fed by a permanently inserted gastroscopy tube to maintain his nutrition, his speech is so incomprehensible that he communicates via a machine displaying his typed messages, and he is, let's face it, a complete wreck as a human being compared with his previous self. He has lost almost everything except his intrinsic humanity, and I must admit that he has shown vastly more bravery and dignity than I would have expected. It just goes to show that you just can't predict how the affected people are going to behave. He can still use his sphincters so he is not incontinent and he can just about make love with his wife. Mind you, James has a very big advantage in that he has a very loving family with a caring and deeply compassionate wife and two children who have literally excelled themselves in their practical help and compassion for everything that their kindly and highly intelligent father has lost. It almost makes me sad. I know I should never feel this way, but I just do from time to time. It is essential that I control that.

JAMES AND NOAH

Veronica, Paul and Clare entered the large rectangular expanse of the hospital's intensive care unit and quickly identified the forlorn sight of James lying in the second bed on the right. They were immediately greeted by a sympathetic and highly trained senior nurse who warned them that his death was only a few hours away at the most. She escorted them to James who was deeply unconscious and unresponsive to any commands or kindly words from his three close relatives. This was surely the end game. Multiple tubes were connected to his emaciated body including intravenous drips in both arms, a urinary catheter and the pre-existing gastroscopy tube connected to his stomach. As might be expected, his breathing was also being assisted by a mechanical ventilator, the regular purring noise of which tended to soothe their nerves instead of frightening them. However, James had made his wishes abundantly clear in writing – he was not to be resuscitated if he had a cardiac arrest, and not to be kept alive on a ventilator if his condition was hopeless which of course it would be in due course. While Veronica was emotionally devastated at the idea of her beloved husband no longer existing, she also respected his stated wishes.

After a further three days of this hopeless support, and after consultation with Veronica, all further treatment was stopped by the medical staff and the ventilator turned off. Within four hours James stopped breathing, his heart gave up and he was pronounced dead.

*

Well there it is. Poor James finally succumbs to my invasion of his nervous system and he is now well and truly dead, so my work is just about done. Of course, his inevitable death also means that I shall soon cease to exist as well, at least in my present form, and from a philosophical point of view, this is just a completion of the natural cycle of life and death. My extinction is an inevitable consequence of my infiltration and destruction of his body. The more I think about it, it is clear that I would not make a very good infectious agent, like a virus or a bacterium, because my host dies without my particular disease being passed on to another host. Such is his lot in life, I keep telling myself, but at least I know that I have fulfilled my awful destiny and done my job well. Congratulations to everyone involved.

SPEAK THE WORD

One of the greatest difficulties in life is to know and fully understand the difference between a true coincidence and a manifestation of the supernatural. While most people are seldom unduly concerned by this distinction, and just choose to rely completely on what they see as simple common sense, there remain a few who are just unable to do this. These latter individuals tend to question almost everything they see with their eyes and experience with all their senses, and, perhaps out of an obsessive notion that the world about them is far more mysterious and complex than generally thought, they almost never dismiss what everyone else thinks is just a coincidence, a matter of no importance or significance. Doctor Ralph Skerrington is just such an unusual person, and what I recount here is the complete truth as he told it to me about three months before his sudden and inexplicable disappearance.

It was, I believe, a warm and sunny June morning when Ralph first became aware of a series of odd coincidences as he was reading one of his favourite literary magazines in his small book-lined scholarly study in an upmarket suburb of south London. Odd though they may have seemed at first, these episodes also had an unusual flavour of familiarity about them, as if this was just a variation of the usual rules of living in an increasingly articulate world. As was entirely normal for him, he also had his small but powerful radio switched on, and the blaring tone and distinctly high-brow conversations that emanated from the old but reliable device sitting neatly on his writing desk did not disturb his reading in the least. Ralph had always been able to do several things at once, and had much greater than average powers of concentration. Indeed, the regular background noise and elegant words coming from the radio were a sort of comfort to him, as if he was not alone in the world. He welcomed the company of strange voices, even if they were transmitted to him by virtual means. It truly helped his sense of isolation. In his London University position as a Reader in English Literature he certainly counted a few of his professional colleagues as friends, but none of them were close to him, and he would never impose anything on them.

The first time it occurred, Ralph thought nothing further about it and just dismissed it as a coincidence. After all, he had heard other people say that exactly the same thing had happened to them on occasion. So he thought, entirely reasonably at the time, that this was just part of daily life. What actually happened is simple. Just as he was reading a particular word in his magazine, he heard exactly the same word uttered by the person speaking on his radio. He remembered well that very first occasion, and the word in question was 'reliable'. Thus, when he read in his periodical that this particular writer was never *reliable* in his everyday dealings with people, he also heard over the radio that in the medical profession it was assumed that the doctors were always *reliable*. He read and heard that word simultaneously. This sort of coincidence happens to just about everyone, including so-called 'normal' people like him, and he really wasn't at all fazed by it. Indeed, he hardly gave it a further thought.

But then it happened a second time, just thirty minutes after the first occasion. He was on page twenty-nine of his literary magazine, about half-way through the entire issue, when he came to read the word 'excessive'. Just as he read that a well-known writer was *excessive* in his demands, he heard at that very moment over the radio that it was important not to *be excessive* in one's attitude to benefits. Again, most people would have dismissed this second event as just another example of simple coincidence, but Ralph was at this stage far more concerned than one might have expected. Indeed, even as I write this, the word 'demands' was both written by me and heard over the radio simultaneously, and I just dismissed this as a coincidence, just as two people at a party might well share the same birthday. But Ralph's mental antennae were far more highly attuned than the rest of us, and he was already beginning to be suspicious. The fact that he had always had an open mind to the sum total of life's experiences must surely have contributed to his reaction to what then occurred.

There were no further episodes of this experience on that June day, though this may well just have been due to Ralph discontinuing his reading of his magazine soon after this odd coincidence which had certainly startled him. But it was a very different story the following morning when he continued reading a modern novel that he had only recently started, and was keen to finish so he could get on with something else. Ralph was never a very patient man, and always seemed to be in a hurry to get things done as quickly as possible. This time the same thing happened when he read the book at the same time as listening to the radio. But it was worse than before in that both written and audible words occurred simultaneously many times over the course of just one hour. At the very moment he read the word *excitable* in his book, he heard someone say *excitable* on the radio. Just a few minutes later the word *forthcoming* was read and heard at the same time. It occurred to Ralph that this was more than just a series of coincidences. Something stranger, perhaps more sinister, was going on in his life. What that mystery was remained completely unknown to him.

As well as being a high level academic, Ralph was also a very logical person, and despite his acknowledged expertise in the Arts, he also had something of a scientific bent. Accordingly, the next day he tried an obvious experiment. He wanted to know whether the same thing might happen if the spoken words emanated from a different medium. His home study contained a small portable television perched at one end of a table adjacent to his main desk. He usually only turned it on to hear the news, but on this occasion, late in the evening after his university daytime work had finished, he pressed the on/off button on the remote device in his hand and saw on the screen a group of politicians arguing among themselves over some current (and in Ralph's view unimportant) issue that was already a hot topic in the country. They frequently talked over each other, making the individual spoken words difficult to make out, but there were still enough words for him to reach a conclusion. He opened his novel at the page he had last read and started to read the small typeface. Somewhat to his surprise, nothing untoward happened for the first two pages. But after that, exactly the same thing as before happened as he continued reading. When he read the word *outstanding* he heard that word spoken by one of the politicians on the television. About one minute later he heard the word *unintentionally* emanate from the television at exactly the same moment that he read that very word in his book. Rather undaunted by this experience he continued his reading, and two minutes later he read the word *given* just as this word was spoken by a person on the television. And so it went on until he had counted at least nine simultaneous examples of this phenomenon over the course of just ten minutes and five pages of the novel. At this point he stopped reading, put the book down on his large desk and switched off the television. There was now very little doubt in his mind. What was occurring in his life could not be written off as just a series of unremarkable coincidences. But as to what was going on, he was still very much in the dark.

The next day he thought of just one more experiment to make him absolutely certain that something extraordinary was revealing itself to him. So he bought a highly regarded broadsheet newspaper in the morning from the local newsagent as he walked to work, and only started to read it later in the afternoon. In his university office he had another radio, though not quite as compact and neat as the one in his house study, and he turned it on. What emanated from the device was ideal for his purpose as it was a current affairs programme with two people having an interesting and intelligent conversation on economics. He opened up the folded newspaper and started to read, slowly. Exactly the same thing happened. Over the course of ten minutes he found that on eleven separate occasions, whenever he heard a particular word uttered on the radio, he was actually reading that same word in his newspaper. So this weird simultaneous merging of the spoken word and the read word occurred in more than just one medium and in more than just one piece of reading material. Though the phenomenon was therefore completely real, Ralph still had two critical questions that needed answers. The first was whether what he was experiencing was a supernatural event, and the second was what he should do next. While he was pretty certain about the answer to the first, he still had no sensible answer to the second.

Since I was at the time working in the same department as Ralph, I saw him from time to time during this most difficult period for him. I had always admired the sheer breadth of his learning which had already resulted in his writing four scholarly and very detailed books on nineteenth-century romantic novelists. I thought that even though he was only thirty-six years of age, nevertheless he was so good that a personal University Chair could not be far off, and he was also a noted teacher who was greatly valued by both his students and his peers. In short, Ralph was definitely a rising star in his field, and, in the opinion of many of his colleagues, including myself, his star had already risen.

During a period which must have spanned several months, the fact that he was suffering from some kind of mental disturbance was pretty obvious to me, as I knew him quite well, but not to the rest of his colleagues in the English department. To my eye, he seemed somewhat distracted but until he actually told me about his problem, I had no idea what it was. But clearly something major was bothering him as his entire demeanour seemed to change, though in rather subtle ways. Normally a rather relaxed individual, he seemed to be increasingly anxious about the slightest thing, and was generally on edge. I am sure his friends, assuming he had any, would have noticed such a change in his normally laid-back personality. He began to worry greatly about reviews of his books, whereas before he did not even bother to read his reviews, so confident was he of his scholarship and mastery of the generalities and specifics of his chosen literary field.

So you can imagine my surprise when one day in the early autumn of that year Ralph invited me to his office and told me what the problem was, and how he had tried to find a rational explanation for all that he had experienced during the previous few months since the middle of summer. He and I had become good friends over the previous two years, and, most important of all, he trusted me and valued my discretion. The only reason why I am now recording his story for posterity is that Ralph is no longer with us.

What actually happened to him I have never been able to discover, though in my own view the most likely reason for his disappearance is that he could no longer cope with this new and frightening dimension to his life. So, he either took his own life or ran away from London and his prestigious post and made a completely different life for himself in some other place, perhaps even another country. Whichever is true, I never saw him again and, to the best of my knowledge, neither did anyone else in our department. Things must have been made easier for him in that he had no close family living with him. He was a single man with, so far as I am aware, no particularly close ties with anyone, be that friend or family.

What may have pushed Ralph over the edge, so to speak? I shall never know for sure but I think he had almost certainly been seriously destabilised by what happened to him next. We have already heard about the simultaneous reading and hearing of particular words, something that when he was in a more rational frame of mind he thought was probably a matter of great coincidence, but at other times he thought was possibly something far more sinister. He decided to try one further experiment to finally settle the matter, though I am sure in retrospect he rather wished he had not done so. With one of his favourite books open at a random page, he uttered the first word that came into his head. He recalled that word as being *justified*. He closed his eyes as he spoke the word and then, with his eyes still closed, he pointed his finger to a random part of the page. To his great surprise and horror his finger pointed to the word *justified*. He repeated this exercise again and again that late summer evening, and in every case the printed word matched his spoken utterances. He then went further, and switched on the small radio in his study. He spoke a particular word at random, initially the word *tomorrow*, and he immediately heard the word *tomorrow* spoken by the male voice emanating from his radio. He repeated this procedure multiple times over the rest of the evening, but in every case the same simultaneous occurrence of words occurred without fail. At this point, so Ralph told me, he was completely convinced that these strange phenomena and experiences just could not be explained by anything other than supernatural forces. I was still somewhat sceptical about this, but he was absolutely convinced, despite his usually rational way of looking at the world and all its oddities.

A few months later, Ralph disappeared from my and everyone else's life for what I assume will be forever. Once an observer of coincidences, he became, in a sense, the master of the spoken word. Or, rather, should he be called its slave?

NOW YOU SEE IT

June and Roger Bergerac were greatly in need of a break away from work and the relentless bustle of London life, exciting as that might be. But the question they asked themselves was exactly where their short vacation should be. While Roger was usually stressed in his senior management position in a large engineering company, June was, in her own way, equally stressed and under constant work and time pressure as a laboratory technician in their local teaching hospital. Already in their mid-fifties, they just felt that they needed to get away from it all and recharge their batteries so to speak before they became too stale and unmotivated to do their respective jobs well. Their two teenage sons were well able to look after themselves during their parents' brief absence, and indeed would no doubt rather enjoy rattling between rooms in the large family house in a distinctly upmarket suburb of England's capital.

But where should they go? After much constructive discussion, laced with a modicum of enthusiasm, sarcasm and negativity on both sides, they finally agreed to spend four days in a small but stylish hotel in a small village just outside Exeter, the capital city of Devon and a place they had always wanted to visit, though tourism was never a major source of income for the city. It would be an experience completely outside their normal routine, and as such it seemed ideal for what they sought.

After the usual preparations, they left London on a Friday morning and drove the two hundred miles to Exeter in just over four hours, a journey that did little to tax their comfortable automatic Mercedes though they were both sorely taxed by motorway tedium. In the late afternoon, they passed through the city of Exeter, which they found particularly, if not rather surprisingly, impressive and drove the remaining few miles to the nearby village which would be their home for four nights. Roger had done his homework with customary precision, and had no difficulty whatsoever in locating the small hotel where they would stay. It was originally an old manor house, located close to the curving main street; constructed in the mid-eighteenth century for landed gentry, it had been tastefully converted into a modern hotel accommodating up to twenty people at any one time. It was still full of character and retained some of the original architectural features, including extensive wooden panelling in the long entry hall and the bannisters that lined the broad staircase leading to the first-floor rooms. The entire internal structure exuded an ambience that was both stylish and atmospheric. It created quite an impression on June and Roger, one that was somehow enhanced by the faintly musty smell, an odd mixture of breakfast, mahogany and old age, which made them feel as if they really were in a very unusual and historical place. They were right to be impressed, but as it turned out, probably for entirely the wrong reasons. Though keen to get a taste of west country hospitality and culture, there is only a certain amount of novel experience that most people can endure, and they were certainly no exception.

The middle-aged and bespectacled woman at the hotel's narrow reception desk was friendly enough without giving the impression of fashionable political correctness, and spoke with a faint but definite west country burr. Despite this, she maintained a curious aura of severity which radiated from her like an invisible power. After Roger had signed his name on the paper document she had given him, she seemed to size them both up carefully before giving them some unsettling but also rather amusing information about the old hotel.

'I'm sure you know this already,' she said to them while moving her head towards Roger in a distinctly conspiratorial fashion, 'but this hotel has been haunted for many years by a ghost.'

'A ghost?' replied June, not without a little amazement.

'Yes, a ghost. We see him from time to time, mainly in the hallway…'

'*Him* did you say?' uttered June, now slightly anxious.

'Yes indeed,' replied the receptionist, whose name was Primrose. 'His name is Barnaby Atkins, and he is said to have died violently at the hands of two local criminals about two hundred years ago. Rumour has it that he was fatally stabbed in the neck.'

Roger was unimpressed by this revelation, and was clearly not as easily scared as his wife. 'So if he died all that time ago, why does he come back as a ghost to haunt the hotel?' he asked Primrose.

'The story goes that he was never properly laid to rest as his remains weren't buried in hallowed ground, so his soul has been left aimlessly wandering the earth, in particular this hotel where he was killed, ever since in the form of a white ghost.'

Roger smiled and addressed her directly, fixing his gaze on her rather dreamlike eyes. 'Do you actually believe all this nonsense or are you just trying to scare your clients, to create an illusion of mystery to add to the hotel's charming ambience and character?'

Primrose did not like this question one bit and looked at Roger rather contemptuously as though he were a doubting Thomas, and a very irritating one at that. But she smiled ruefully as if she was addressing a naughty schoolchild and replied politely. 'Oh it's all true you know. Of course Barnaby's ghost only reveals itself to certain people who are somehow receptive, and he only appears in the hotel from time to time.'

'When was the last sighting?' asked June, who was clearly a little concerned.

'About six weeks ago as I recall,' was the reply, 'but you needn't worry. Even if you see Barnaby's ghost, you won't be in any danger whatsoever. No-one has ever been physically hurt...'

'*Physically* hurt you say?' said June.

'That's right. Mind you, I have to admit that now and again some guests do get rather spooked, if you know what I mean. Actually, a few months ago a couple saw the ghost and then suddenly checked out two days early because they were so scared... but they were OK, so you don't need to worry even if you see him.'

'Thank you,' said Roger, 'I find that very reassuring.'

Primrose detected a hint of sarcasm in his voice. But there the conversation came to a halt.

Primrose smiled warmly at them and gave Roger the two plastic cards that they would need to enter their assigned bedroom, adding her wish that they would both enjoy the sumptuous dinner that was waiting for them later that evening in the hotel's surprisingly large dining room. It was adorned with tall curtains, a deep and rich red in colour, antique wooden furniture and many old paintings of previous hotel proprietors and other notable figures from the past. There were no pictures, however, of Barnaby Atkins.

*

As promised by Primrose, the delicious four-course dinner that evening was more than sumptuous, in fact it was probably one of the finest meals that either Roger or June had ever had. Even the red wine that accompanied it was remarkably fruity and refreshing. There were few other diners in the elegant dining room which surprised them both somewhat, but as paying guests that was hardly their problem. Suitably satiated, and in remarkably good spirits, helped no doubt by the effects of the strong red wine, they stood up, just a little unsteadily, and began to survey the hotel's antique charm. Roger had his newly purchased and extremely expensive camera placed snugly inside his left jacket pocket, and decided to take just a few photographs of the elegantly panelled hallway and staircase. He was keen to have a permanent record of the ambience that they both found so charming and enticing.

Roger's camera was, naturally, a digital device and he was able to immediately view the many photographs he had just taken. Coupled devices had changed the art of photography forever and to a much greater extent than anyone had ever thought possible. He could still, just about, remember a time when one had to buy a roll of camera film, comprising either twenty of thirty-six pictures, and have it developed to see the results. The few days waiting could be almost unbearable. In previous days, few things were so instantaneous, and one consequence of this remarkable advance is that everyone, including Roger and June, now takes numerous photographs of an object or vista in the hope that at least a few of them might live up to their high expectations. When behind a camera, just about everyone considers themselves experts.

But, as it turned out, it took only one photograph on Roger's camera to permanently destabilise them both. In retrospect, he cursed the day he decided to use his camera inside the hotel. It is said that the camera never lies. That may well be true in many senses, but they both wished that in this particular case such a truism was actually false. It all started so innocently, much like most disasters in life (and also in death). The first few photographs Roger took showed nothing untoward, just a clear vision of the wooden panelling of the hallway walls. But when he looked at the fifth picture, he saw something that was totally unexpected and which made him seriously worried. When he pressed the button on his camera to view the image he had just taken, he saw a definite vision, though rather vague and grey-white, of what looked like a man but without a clear demarcation of his legs. Indeed he appeared to be legless and was dressed in a long white gown. Just enough of the head was visible to allow Roger to think that the image was of a man rather than a woman or child. He had no doubt whatsoever that his camera had captured an image of a ghost, and he thought immediately of what Primrose had told them both about the ghost of Barnaby Atkins. He began to think she was right after all – *seeing is believing* so the saying goes. That was probably true as well.

His immediate reaction was to show the picture to June, mainly to convince himself that he wasn't hallucinating. The wine they had just consumed with such relish was certainly strong stuff, but surely it wasn't that powerful! But showing June the photo only made him seriously scared and perplexed as she was able to see only the elegant hallway, and not the grey-white vision of what Roger reckoned must surely be Barnaby's ghost. She saw nothing untoward, absolutely nothing that even resembled a ghost. He and his wife were different people, who, despite their shared values and insights, still had differing perceptions, world views, emotional capabilities, and indeed thresholds for believing what they see with their own eyes.

'But surely you can see the strange human form in the picture?' Roger pleaded.

The answer from June was as clear as day. 'I'm sorry Roger, but your eyes must be playing tricks on you. I can't see anything of the kind.'

They agreed to disagree, and Roger told her that he would not look at the photographs on his camera again that evening, but that they would both look again the next morning.

'When the effects of the wine have worn off and after a good night's sleep I'm absolutely sure you won't see anything other than the wooden staircase and hallway,' she told him.

'I'm sure you're right as usual,' Roger admitted to his wife.

*

As soon as he woke up the following morning, Roger felt an overwhelming compulsion to look at the images on his camera. While he hoped that the ghostly image might be absent, to his horror he found that it was still there in all its frightening and supernatural reality.

'Oh dear, oh dear,' he said to June, 'the bloody thing is still there.'

June was still groggy from a good night's sleep.

'What's there Roger?' she managed to ask.

'The white ghost of Barnaby Atkins, of course,' he replied, already quite irritated both with his camera and his wife.

'Oh that… are you sure?'

'Of course, it's still there in one of the photos.'

June quickly became more alert and asked to see the picture on her husband's camera. Roger showed her the offending image and she just shook her head in disbelief. 'All I can see is the elegant hallway… I can't see anything else and certainly not any damn ghost.'

'Well I can see it… I hope I'm not going mad.'

At this, June started to feel alarmed and tried to reassure him. 'Look,' she told him, 'don't be silly. I don't know what's going on here but what you're suggesting just doesn't make sense. Ghosts don't exist in reality, only in people's minds.'

Roger looked at her quizzically. He was certain he didn't want an argument. 'OK,' he admitted, 'maybe you're right. I'll take some more pictures of the hallway after breakfast and hopefully none of them will show anything frightening.'

This was exactly what he did right after consuming a remarkably good hot breakfast which put them both in a particularly good mood. When he examined the twelve photographs he'd just taken with the same small camera, all of them were unremarkable and none of them showed anything that could be remotely construed as looking like a ghost. Both of them were considerably relieved. To be even more reassured, June also took several photographs of the hotel's elegant hallway, and none of them showed anything unexpected. So Roger began to relax.

'Of course this place could still be haunted,' Roger remarked. 'Maybe the ghost of Barnaby Atkins only appears to certain people in the evenings and not during the hours of daylight, such as they are.'

'Oh come off it, Roger. That's just buying into the whole supernatural myth.'

'OK, point taken.'

*

Later that day, and during the three days that remained of their holiday, Roger and June explored the countryside surrounding the main city and were greatly impressed with both the beauty of what they saw and the friendliness of almost all the people they met. They took dozens of photographs of the city of Exeter and all the beauty spots and buildings of historical interest within the area, and all of them reproduced only what they were designed to.

The brief vacation was over even before they were able to truly relax, but the break had certainly lowered their mutual stress levels which had been raised to a dangerous degree by their respective workplaces. So overall, they felt the whole excursion had been a good idea, despite the strange and inexplicable episode with Roger's camera, a distinctly unsettling experience for both of them, and one which, fortunately, was not repeated.

Soon after they arrived back in their large, detached house in the Highgate region of London, Roger could not resist looking at the pictures on his camera again. Once settled comfortably in his well-appointed study, he transferred all of the photographs he had taken in Devon to his laptop computer, creating a new photos folder as he did so. After he had done this, he erased all the pictures from their recent vacation from his camera, including the one showing the putative ghost. When he opened the computer folder, he easily managed to identify the offending ghostly image amongst the many innocent photographs he had taken and then transferred. As far as he was concerned, he had his suspicions about the provenance of the one frightening image but he decided to say no more about it to June. It just wasn't worth it. The image of Barnaby Atkins, or whoever it was, if anyone, could stay hidden in his laptop computer forever so far as he was concerned. It was best to let sleeping dogs lie, and anyway, neither of them had been physically harmed in any way.

The next day, however, which he had taken off from work in advance, he found that his computer was malfunctioning. While this had happened before on a number of occasions, this time the problem somehow seemed different and more serious. Suspecting a computer virus, although it seemed unlikely in view of his anti-virus software, he checked the system with the virus tracker software; as he expected, a computer virus was not the cause. The main problem was that he was unable to save any new documents, something that caused him great frustration, especially as he was unable to save a four-page work report that he had just spent two hours composing. While Roger generally tried hard to avoid uttering expletives, on this occasion he uttered a whole string of them as he just couldn't control his anger. He then opened the folder containing all his holiday photographs, including the offending image. To his surprise, and his relief, the photograph only showed the elegant hotel hallway, along with its stylish wooden panelling – there was no evidence whatsoever of the ghost or whatever the figure was. He began to think that his wife was right and that he had imagined it all, maybe as a consequence of all the work stress he had been under, not to mention his distinct tendency towards neuroticism. But the more he tried to use his laptop, the more things seemed to go wrong. For example, he only had intermittent access to the internet despite a very good wifi system in the house, and his internet searches were only occasionally successful. Roger began to wonder what exactly was going on, if anything, and started to become just a little fearful for the first time rather than just very curious.

He immediately relayed all this information and his difficulties to June who, not surprisingly, dismissed the whole thing as just bad luck and nothing more sinister than that. But for the first time she became genuinely concerned that her normally sensible and well-balanced husband was beginning to lose the plot and become truly irrational. Roger, who was not an unintelligent or insensitive man, perceived a subtle change in his wife's demeanour towards him and again checked the photos folder. But there was no evidence whatsoever of the offending image.

Meanwhile, June, acting on an impulse, decided to open her own laptop and transferred all her camera photographs to a designated computer folder which she called 'Devon holiday photos'. But, to her complete amazement, when she looked at the very first photo she had taken of the wooden panelled corridor, she saw a clear image of her husband. In it he looked both frightened and startled and she was taken aback to say the least. But there was no evidence of the grey-white ghost that had so spooked him. But now she herself was pretty spooked. Since she was aware of Roger's problems with his own computer, she decided to connect to the internet, but as had happened with Roger's computer, the whole system malfunctioned and appeared to be broken. She was also completely unable to save any new documents. Whatever she tried to do with her computer, the entire system just failed.

While June was trying hard to make sense of everything that had happened over the previous four days, and all that was happening to them both in the present moment, Roger walked into her small study with a broad smile across his face. 'Guess what?' he said to her.

'I have no idea,' June replied, completely perplexed and almost defeated.

'Well I don't know what I just did, but somehow my computer has completely corrected itself, and it's now working perfectly.'

June gave him a doleful look and for the first time she was absolutely convinced that at least one of them was deranged.

A QUESTION OF STATISTICS

The Reverend Jonas Simmons, MA, BD, had only just finished his generous eulogy for the recently deceased Roderick Wiltonshire when a dark cloud appeared right above the churchyard and threatened to ruin the entire event. Rod, as he liked to be called, was only fifty-seven years old when he died, somewhat unexpectedly, just a week before the solemn Church of England funeral, but Reverend Simmons had put on a really good show. Rod's stunned widow, Jean, and his two grieving teenage daughters, Alice and Zoe, were well pleased with the stirring send-off that the wise and kind local church minister had given their husband and father. For sure it was a deeply sad occasion, and the shockwaves were still reverberating after Rod's sudden death, but there was still just a hint of misguided optimism from his wife that he may have gone to a better place, a higher plane of existence, or, more likely in his children's view, to a stark void of absolutely nothing except total oblivion, destined to remain just a memory in the minds of the few people who actually knew or cared about him.

The rest of the funeral did not take very long, and Rod's coffin was slowly lowered into the designated grave at a far end of the cemetery as the assembled crowd of family, his few friends, work colleagues, acquaintances, and a few hangers on who just loved solemn occasions, looked on with either genuine or feigned sympathy. Jean, red-eyed from crying and grief, just wanted the whole thing to be over and done with. The general opinion was that the ceremony had gone off as well as could possibly be expected. Mercifully, though it was mid-February and the sky was still ominously grey and dark, it did not rain or snow and the day was remarkably mild. However, the sun did not shine even once during the proceedings.

The ironic thing about Rod was that he never expected to die in the first place, certainly not at fifty-seven years of age, and, if we are to be completely frank about it, preferably not ever. No-one really expects to die, whatever they may say to themselves, family and friends. And when they do, it always comes as a great shock to just about everyone, including the person themself, assuming he or she is even aware of it which on logical grounds seems highly unlikely. But, of course, one never knows that for sure. No-one has ever been able to tell us what actually happens at such a landmark occasion in their lives.

Rod had a degree in history from a respectable new 'red brick' university, and after ten years in the food industry, he had eventually found work as a middle manager in a prestigious London teaching hospital, with a primary responsibility for the procurement of essential equipment for the hospital's somewhat demanding surgeons. He was happily and stably married to Jean, an extremely kind as well as attractive woman, and was also very fond of his two teenage daughters. Whether they were equally fond of him remains an open question. But he had an obsession about living, which was perhaps increased because of his interaction with knowledgeable members of the medical profession on a daily basis. He wanted to live a long life, well into his nineties just as his father and maternal grandfather had done. Because of this desire, he did everything he could to increase the statistical chances of his living to a ripe old age. He seemed to be concerned less with the actual quality of his life than with its length. While not particularly ambitious in his professional life, though he was well-respected and liked by most of his peers and medical colleagues, he showed great ambition in his personal life in so far as he wanted to keep healthy and active for as long as humanly possible. To live to anything less than ninety years old was just not good enough. To kick the bucket, so to speak, even in his eighties, as his own mother had done, just would not do.

So what was the plan that would ensure his obsessional desire to live a long time became a reality?

Well, so it seemed to Rod, it all boiled down to a question of statistics. While he was no clever actuary, nevertheless, as a medically knowledgeable man, he knew enough about maintaining a healthy lifestyle to load the dice in his favour. The main problem, or so it seemed to his wife and children, was that he took his obsession too seriously and seemed to try just a little too hard to realise his rather irrational dream of longevity.

Rod had a logical and well-organised mind and decided that his best chance of living to at least ninety was to engage in a profoundly healthy lifestyle, something that he regretted he had not paid sufficient attention to in his youth and early middle age. While all of the measures he decided to take would certainly increase his general well-being and chances of long-term survival, he was forgetting that a critical factor in longevity was to choose one's parents with care. Both of his parents had lived until at least their early eighties so he was quite well placed to live for quite a long time. But even healthy living can't protect a person from random mutations in one's DNA, changes which could increase his chances of getting cancer, for example. He had no control over this possibility so, quite sensibly, he didn't worry about or factor it into his estimations. Rod might be a neurotic obsessional, but he was not a complete ignoramus. Though some of his close family might disagree on that one.

So Rod devised a plan and, it has to be said, it wasn't a bad one by any means. He stood exactly five foot nine inches in his bare feet and he maintained an ideal weight for his height to ensure a BMI of twenty-one which was slim normal. If he showed the slightest deviation from this weight then he would adjust his food intake and exercise regime accordingly. Regarding his eating habits, they became the most obsessional aspect of his lifestyle, and his diet was by no means inexpensive. He insisted on his wife feeding him the regulation five portions of vegetables and fruit per day, a regime that he adhered to rigidly, despite the cost as he would insist on only the highest quality of food. He really ought to have ensured that his entire family ate as healthily as he did but there was no evidence of this, yet another testimony to his complete selfishness and lack of concern for those closest to him. Despite the controversy about red wine having beneficial effects on the heart and in preventing strokes, he also drank one small glass of the highest quality red wine every evening as he was a true believer. He avoided sugar-rich foods like biscuits, cakes, white bread and high-calorie soft drinks like the plague, but he did allow himself the luxury of one square of ninety per cent dark chocolate every day because it contained antioxidants. He also studiously avoided consuming foods high in saturated fat such as butter, cheese and full fat milk. Instead, he always ate cholesterol-lowering polyunsaturated margarine, brown wholemeal bread and skimmed milk.

He was well aware of the benefits of regular exercise, so he did a vigorous hour-long exercise regime in the local gym three times a week. He just couldn't face gym work every day, but he did walk very fast every evening for thirty minutes in his local neighbourhood. Because of this he had an excellent exercise tolerance and had never experienced either chest pain or breathlessness during strenuous exercise. One thing he did not do was jog as he had once tried this and found it extremely boring and potentially dangerous in that joggers risked being run over by inattentive car drivers. In order to maintain some degree of flexibility with his increasing age, he also devised a twenty-minute yoga regime that he adhered to rigidly every evening. Naturally, he had paid privately for a full health screen which had included an electrocardiogram (ECG), and an exercise ECG, both of which were entirely normal. The screen had also included a full serum lipid profile which was highly satisfactory. His total cholesterol was normal, his 'good' high density lipoprotein was way above normal, his 'bad' low density lipoprotein was normal, and the ratio of total cholesterol to high density lipoprotein was 2.6 which was perfect. Furthermore, Rod had never smoked, there was no family history of heart disease or stroke, and he was on no medications. He was also free of any medical conditions such as diabetes or hypertension. He was sure of the latter as he had bought a portable sphygmomanometer to measure his blood pressure, and he and Jean would measure each other's blood pressure with great precision every three months. His blood pressure never went above 120/80 even when he felt very anxious. Perhaps most importantly, he was not particularly stressed in his work. So, all things considered, Rod was a pretty good bet for a long and healthy life. He had made sure of it. His family were somewhat bemused by all these patently self-obsessed activities, but they tolerated his rather bizarre behaviour both because Rod was an intrinsically decent man, and also because they all saw a good deal of common sense in their husband or father maintaining his good health.

But even all of these precautionary measures were not enough for him. He needed to get some kind of external validation of what he was doing to himself. So he went to the internet for assistance. Not entirely surprisingly, he began to access a whole variety of 'how long will you live?' questionnaires. While some of these were written in the United Kingdom, others, usually the more detailed ones, originated from the USA. The first few British questionnaires revealed to him that his estimated death was eighty-four years.

Now that displeased him as that estimate just would not do. He wanted more. But even when he retook the survey and altered various parameters, it made no difference. The only manoeuvres that increased his estimated lifespan were to change his sex or location, and there was nothing that he could do, or indeed was prepared to do, about those. He had more luck with the detailed American questionnaires that estimated how long he was likely to live. These generally predicted a lifespan upwards of ninety years, with one even going so far as telling him that given his healthy lifestyle and favourable family history, he was probably on course for living until the ripe old age of ninety-seven years, just like one of his grandparents. Well, he said to himself, that was more like it! In future he would only refer to these American 'how long will you live?' websites, and not the less favourably disposed ones.

So this was how Rod lived his life in his mid-fifties. His obsession soon developed into a natural way of carrying on, and everything he did to keep healthy just became a part of his normal life, adapted into a rigorous regime that hardly ever varied from day to day. That was also accepted, somewhat reluctantly it must be said, by his long-suffering wife and two teenage children. It never occurred to Rod that his behaviour was just a little pathetic.

But a few months after he first accessed the 'how

long will you live?' questionnaires, he somewhat absent-mindedly went for a brisk walk along the streets near his home in Highgate. With his mind fixed on something else, and certainly not on the roads in front of him, he failed to see a large lorry, weighing at least twenty tonnes, hurtling towards him at great speed along the road that he was about to cross. He was not at a much safer zebra crossing. Rod did not pay sufficient attention to his immediate surroundings and moved forwards without looking to the left or the right. In a matter of seconds he was hit by the rapidly advancing lorry just as he stepped onto the road. He was, unsurprisingly, killed instantly. It never occurred to him during life that all one can do is give an estimate of a person's projected lifespan, a statistical likelihood for certain, but nothing more than that. Statistics are all well and good but can never anticipate a lethal traumatic event. Rod would have been better off just living his life rather than worrying about it.

PAST AND PRESENT

Jacob Remington is obsessed with the past, particularly the middle of the eighteenth century. He has a stable job as a well-respected Senior Lecturer in History at his local red brick university, and has written two favourably reviewed books on key political events during this period over two hundred and fifty years ago. His considerate and long-suffering wife Jessica is well used to her husband's eccentricities and has never been unduly concerned with his consuming obsession with the past. After all, he has an interesting and respectable position in academia, is a generous provider for his close-knit family, a good and loyal husband, a fine father to their three children, and is a generally kind and decent human being. The only problem, which initially escaped Jessica's attention, is that Jacob is just a little mad.

Whenever Jacob waxes lyrical about the glorious eighteenth century, Jessica gently reminds him of all the medical advantages of modern life such as antibiotics, anaesthesia, vaccinations and a generally high standard of dental care, none of which were available in the seventeen hundreds. People actually died pretty often from conditions such as simple streptococcal infections and bacterial pneumonia. Even childbirth could be a very risky business because of a lack of medical and nursing care and the dreaded puerperal fever that carried away so many unfortunate women just after birth because antibiotics were not available until the early nineteen forties which was two hundred years later. As for the appallingly high incidence of infant mortality, this is almost impossible to imagine.

While he takes all these points on board, nevertheless he still secretly, or perhaps not so secretly, desires to live as a well-off gentleman of two hundred and fifty years ago. The truth is that he finds life in the early twenty-first century rather boring and monotonous. Obviously, they both know full well that time travel to the past is a physical impossibility. Convincing evidence for this was once uttered by that brilliant physicist and mathematician Stephen Hawking who pointed out that if time travel to the past was actually possible then we should have seen several travellers from the future and, so far as we are aware, that has never happened (assuming they aren't keeping their true provenance to themselves and have maintained absolute secrecy which seems very unlikely). Of course, time travel to the future remains a real possibility one day, either from advances in cryogenic science or as a consequence of space travellers returning to the earth who, because of the laws of special relativity formulated by Einstein, will have aged far less than those people still on earth, including their own children, who would seem like grandparents to them.

There is no getting away from it: Jacob genuinely wishes that he had been born some time in the eighteenth century, preferably around the seventeen forties. He is quite aware of the lack of medical knowledge and widespread quackery, not to mention the appalling attitudes that prevailed at that time regarding the role of women and the curse of slavery; nevertheless, he is willing, somewhat grudgingly it is only fair to say, to bear these travesties of justice if it also means that he can be living at that time. When he thinks of the many great figures in science, medicine, philosophy, music, art, politics, the military and literature who managed to grace the eighteenth century, he finds it possible in his mind to think of it as an even greater period of history than the two centuries of his own time – the twentieth and twenty-first. He just has to consider such world icons as Priestley, Hunter, Hume, Reynolds, Jefferson, Nelson and Goethe to think that his point of view is right – and these names are just a few of the many great figures of that period.

While he fully accepts that his current time has seen enormous advances in medicine and surgery, not to mention the complete change in people's social attitudes towards gender, race and religion, he also thinks of the terrible human cost of two world wars in which many millions of people died, including the totally innocent, not to mention the appalling genocide of the Jewish people by the astonishingly evil Nazis and the ongoing threat of a nuclear conflict that might destroy human civilisation as we know it. Overall then, Jacob has convinced himself that if he ever had a choice, which of course he won't, then he would have preferred to have lived in the past, specifically in the eighteenth century in England, preferably as a well-off citizen, or even as a member of the aristocracy, perhaps with an interest in the natural sciences as a 'gentleman scientist'. The world has always been a dangerous place, and in Jacob's view the dangers of living in the eighteenth century were no greater overall than those of the current times. The real difference lies in the actual nature of those dangers. The key issue, both for him and his wife, is that he is quite serious about all this, and his somewhat unorthodox beliefs are genuinely held.

Perhaps inevitably, there comes a time when he decides to take his obsession with the past a definite step further, rather than just writing about it. The first indication of this change happens out of the blue at a time when Jessica least expects it. It is a balmy mid-summer evening in south London where they live, and it is still light outside as the days are long and bright, quite unlike the depressing darkness and cold of the winter months in England. Unable to locate him outside the large house in their extensive garden she searches the house and in due course enters his heavily book-lined study. She is truly shocked by what she sees. She finds him dressed to the nines in Georgian mid-eighteenth century attire. He is wearing a brown tricorn hat, an elegant white shirt with frilly cuffs, a neat white stock covering his neck, a brown, closely fitting waistcoat, light brown breeches and an elegant pair of silver buckled shoes. Over this he is wearing a long dark brown frock coat which appears to fit him very well. Where he has managed to obtain all of this ancient garb she really has no idea. Perhaps he has contacts in the theatre industry of whom she has remained blissfully unaware. Most perplexing of all for her, when she discovers him in this outfit, is that he isn't at all fazed, a reaction which of itself seems seriously odd to her.

'Jacob, why are you all dressed up like that?' she asks him, quietly.

'Why shouldn't I be?' is his surprised reply.

'But you're wearing the clothes of an eighteenth-century dandy.'

'No,' Jacob corrects her, 'actually, an eighteenth-century nobleman or aristocrat.'

'I see.'

'Oh do you? That's good then, isn't it?'

Jessica feels it is best to humour him as he is clearly slightly, if not severely, deranged. 'Yes absolutely,' she replies. 'And where did you get those elegant clothes?'

'But these are my clothes,' Jacob replies, as if surprised by such an absurd question.

'I see… yes, of course. Anyway, you look very elegant.'

'Thank you Jessica. I also feel very comfortable.'

'I'm glad to hear it,' she says, increasingly convinced that there is something very odd about her erstwhile sensible husband.

*

They do not discuss this strange episode again, and Jessica is happy that Jacob appears to be more or less back to his normal self the next morning. Whether or not he has any clear recollection of this bizarre dressing-up episode she never finds out, but it is certainly enough to make her seriously worried about her husband's mental state. She just hopes that somehow he will grow out of this obsession with the past and focus more on the events of the present time, worrying as they are.

Jacob is perfectly able to carry on in his university

role, and indeed his senior colleagues are sufficiently pleased with his academic performance and teaching results that they encourage him to apply for a readership in history which is a very respectable position for a man of just forty years of age. They anticipate that he will get a university professorship by the time he is forty-five, unless, of course, he is poached by another university and is appointed to a history chair somewhere else. His bosses do not want that to happen as they have a high opinion of both his historical scholarship and his commitment to his chosen subject, an enthusiasm that is readily communicated to all his students who both like him and yet think him to be a trifle unusual. The students are right to think of him in those terms and have sussed out his character rather more accurately than his various colleagues in the department.

Three months after his wife discovers him prancing in his home study in eighteenth-century attire, Jacob suddenly goes missing from home. It is now early autumn, and he just hasn't come home one evening after work. Normally his hours of work are pretty standard and he is almost always back at home for supper around six o'clock in the evening. Jessica is initially not too worried about this, as it once happened before in the early years of their marriage, but when he doesn't come home at all that night she begins to get seriously concerned about his mental state and welfare. It is so unlike him to do this and she begins to fear the worst. Perhaps he has met with an accident or even been robbed or abducted. The possibilities of something terrible having happened to him are endless and intensely worrying. But just as she is about to alert the police to her husband's sudden disappearance the following morning, Jacob turns up at the house, opens the front door with his key and looks at his wife intensely while at the same time shaking his head in either disbelief or disappointment. He is dressed in his regular work clothes, entirely appropriate for an English autumn, and not, thank goodness, in eighteenth-century attire which comes somewhat as a blessing as far as Jessica is concerned.

But he seems quite distressed for some reason and when Jessica gently questions him as to where he's been all this time, he gives her an unexpected answer.

'I've been to the city of London in the year seventeen forty-nine of course.'

Jessica is naturally astonished at what Jacob has told her but decides that it will be prudent to humour him a little. 'I see Jacob, of course,' she says. 'And how long did you stay there?'

He replies immediately and not without a hint of irritation. 'I was there for three weeks as you must know.'

'I see, just three weeks?'

'Yes, that's right, and to be frank, I wish it had been less.'

'And why is that Jacob, if you don't mind me asking?'

Jacob sits down in the large wooden chair in the long hall and answers after a brief pause. 'Well the truth is that I just didn't enjoy my stay there. London was absolutely filthy and stank of human excrement and God knows what else. Also, I was appalled at how easy it was to die there of what we would call relatively minor illnesses…'

'Such as?'

'Well, people died of simple bacterial infections like erysipelas and if you were unlucky enough to catch pneumonia then you'd be fortunate to survive. I mean there were no antibiotics, no anaesthetics so operations were indescribably painful and dangerous to life, and vaccinations hardly existed apart from Dr Jenner's cowpox vaccine to protect from smallpox. And talking of the pox, you just wouldn't believe how many people in all strata of society were riddled with venereal diseases, especially syphilis. It was awful to witness. And as for slavery and the appalling way in which women were treated in the eighteenth century, words just fail me.'

Jessica feels oddly relieved to hear this despite the rest of his story which she just doesn't believe. 'Was there anything else you didn't like Jacob?'

'Yes indeed. Life in mid-eighteenth-century London was profoundly boring, probably even more boring than everyday life in the twenty-first century.'

'Boring you said?'

'Yes, boring for certain, and also very uncomfortable and dangerous. And by the way, God help you if you developed toothache as the only option was to have the tooth pulled. Just forget about any notion of filling a cavity like modern dentists do.'

Jessica decides to continue humouring him and gently takes his coat and briefcase and leads him into their modern kitchen where she makes him poached eggs on toast, one of his favourite breakfast meals.

While he is sleeping in their well-appointed living room, Jessica feels compelled to enter his study because she knows that he must have emptied the contents of his leather briefcase. She feels slightly uneasy about invading what has become, over the years, his personal domain, but she notices a medium-sized book lying in a prominent position on his mahogany desk. She picks it up and opens it to view the contents. The book is called *Tom Jones* and is written by Henry Fielding, an author whose name is certainly familiar to her. But when she looks more closely, she notices that it is not a modern reproduction as there is nothing whatsoever to suggest it is a facsimile of the famous novel. Even more perplexing is the fact that it is clearly a first edition dated seventeen forty-nine, the date of Jacob's so-called sojourn. But it is in perfect, indeed mint, condition with no signs at all of age or foxing. Clearly it has only recently been published. It is as inexplicable as it is disconcerting. She is even more confused than before. Jacob has told her that life in the middle of the eighteenth century in London was actually boring and dangerous, a view that coincides with what she has always believed. But how could he know and how did he acquire that book? Has it been perfectly preserved for over two hundred and seventy years or was it really only just published?

She tries hard not to think too much about the implications of what she has just witnessed. Let sleeping dogs lie, she tells herself, however crazy they may be.

NO REDEMPTION

Jane Exmouth began to feel just a little dizzy as her grandfather's coffin was slowly lowered into the hollow grave that had been so carefully dug for him. Her brother James, two years her senior and putting on a remarkably brave face, immediately sensed his sister's sudden distress and put his right arm gently around her neck and right shoulder in a successful attempt to comfort her in this moment of shared grief for a much-loved member of the family. Knowing that one's grandfather has died at the age of eighty years after a short illness is one thing, but it is quite another to witness the hard reality of the end of a life, an end so stark and final. It just seemed too much to absorb in all its brutality. More time was needed both to appreciate the cruel termination of a life well-lived and to finally accept the sad loss of a relative.

The entire funeral ceremony, from the panegyric eulogies delivered by the kindly minister, friends and family members to the actual burial in his final resting place, lasted little more than an hour, but even that was far too long for his grieving widow, children and grandchildren. Hermann Braski was dead and that was that. Life must go on without him, however difficult that might seem so soon after his passing. In a curious way, almost spiritual in nature, matters were eased somewhat and somehow put into some kind of perspective by the beautiful July weather and the exquisitely maintained grass expanses, interspersed with majestic oak trees and multi-coloured flowers, all visible for hundreds of yards all around the enclosed church cemetery.

Hermann Braski was originally a German national but manged to escape to England in 1944 in order to flee from Nazi Germany which he abhorred even though he was not Jewish but a Lutheran Christian. He loved his new country and took UK citizenship in 1955 and married an English woman called Elizabeth Livingstone with whom he had three children, two girls and a boy, all of whom had successful careers as a chartered accountant, general practitioner in a nearby village, and a documentary film maker. All three of them were also happily married which was as much a blessing to their parents as were their high-flying and stable careers. When Hermann died, he had a total of five grandchildren, all of whom he adored unconditionally, and this warmth was reciprocated by all of them. He had worked as a highly successful local businessman, becoming the CEO of a firm making semi-conductors, was a very strong supporter of his local village council in the south-west country of England, and was also a regular churchgoer. He had given generously to several charities as well as to his local church, and he had a wide circle of friends. He had a particular affinity for people of the Jewish faith including several rabbis with whom he liked to discuss matters of God and religious faith. His charitable work had even earned him an MBE for services to business and charity in his late sixties, a national honour of which both he and his family were extremely proud. While always rather sceptical and cynical about the unequal distribution of national gongs, especially to second-rate political cronies, when Hermann himself was the recipient of such an award he did not even hesitate to accept it. In some way, this high-level recognition helped to seal his role as a local pillar of the British countryside establishment. In spite of this, or maybe because of, he took considerable pains to retain the distinct traces of his natural German accent.

Whenever someone dies in a family, especially if they have had quite a long life, there is always a plethora of distinctly boring jobs that have to be done by someone in the family 'to sort things out'. In the case of Hermann, two of his five grandchildren, Jane and James, whom he adored perhaps even more than the other three, were given the tedious task by their busy mother, a certain Dr Marjorie Billington who was a well-respected local family doctor, of sifting through their late grandfather's papers and memorabilia, most of which were stored in several large cardboard boxes in the attic conversion in their maternal grandparents' house in the rather fashionable city of Cheltenham. Well, thought James, someone has got to do it, and it may as well be him, helped of course by his younger sister to whom he was very close. At that time they were both teenagers, he was nineteen while his sister was seventeen. Herman's widow, who was, not surprisingly, severely grieving at her loss and also angry at the way in which he had been so cruelly taken away from her by pancreatic cancer, had encouraged them to sort through his papers and, if possible, organise them in a logical way, something that in life Hermann had always failed to do for some reason. He was usually a very well organised and methodical person in most matters. Indeed, such a highly attuned sense of order was one of his defining characteristics.

The two teenagers really didn't know what to expect when they got down to the tedious business of sorting out their late grandfather's papers, and scarcely knew where to begin so massive was the task they had before them. This was not helped by the fact that he was known to be a hoarder who seldom threw anything away. Jane rather thought they might find some of Hermann's old love letters especially as he was apparently a rather dashing and handsome man in his younger days, good looks that disappeared remarkably quickly as he settled in his new country at the end of the war. No-one could ever quite understand that, but in his middle age and old age he had assumed the role of a senior citizen with relish and little, if any, regret, and he literally radiated the persona of a much travelled and distinguished grey eminence, an appearance that was enhanced by his sporting an elegant grey beard that covered much of his distinguished face. Yet much as she might search, Jane could find no evidence of anything salacious such as old love letters written either by him or to him by adoring young women. Of course they both realised that absence of evidence is not evidence of absence, and their failure to uncover such romantic secrets in no way meant that Hermann did not have any lovers, or at least some female admirers in his youth.

On the second day of their sorting-out task they uncovered something surprising at the bottom of one of the boxes – some papers that were almost hidden below a bunch of relatively recent photographs of three of his grandchildren, taken when they were all toddlers. What they found in their search were five pages of neat typescript on faded yellow writing paper of about three hundred names without any explanation. Most of the typed names had a pencil tick written by hand neatly beside them. The names were all clearly German, but Jane, who was a particularly astute young woman who was currently studying German for her impending Advanced Level examinations, thought that most of the names looked as if they were Jewish. This was a real surprise to both of them. They had no idea of the significance of this list. However, one day later, as they continued their sorting out of the numerous papers, James uncovered a surprising bombshell. He discovered, wrapped carefully within a large piece of brown cloth, what was clearly a Nazi arm band. There was no doubt about it – it consisted of the well-known SS pattern with a black swastika within a white circle, with a red background and a straight black border at the top and bottom of the band. An awful thought occurred to them both – had their beloved grandfather in reality been a Nazi or perhaps a Nazi sympathiser during the Second World War? Or did he just keep this piece of memorabilia as some kind of misguided souvenir? But what added to their concern was the five-page list of Jewish names. Was this a list of people who had been condemned to die in the concentration camps? Surely that couldn't be the case. It was just unthinkable. They found the very idea of their wonderful and gentle grandfather being an ex-Nazi absolutely absurd.

They agreed not to tell either their parents or their grieving grandmother about what they had found, but decided to contact the Simon Wiesenthal Center and show them both an old and a recent photograph of Hermann and the five-page list of German Jewish names which they had wisely photocopied. They did not expect anything untoward to emerge from this enquiry, but they felt compelled to take things further, if only out of curiosity – and if there was bad news, they would rather know it sooner than later. But they truly expected nothing unpleasant, no unexpected skeletons from Hermann's past to materialise. Wisely, they kept their activities and suspicions to themselves and let no-one else in the family or elsewhere know. Perhaps in retrospect they should have shared their discoveries with someone else. Accordingly, they sent their letter of enquiry together with the document and photographs to the Simon Wiesenthal Center in Los Angeles, in California, USA. They sent the letter by recorded delivery which cost them an exorbitant amount, but this needed to be done and dusted for everyone's sake. If any organisation could uncover a murky Nazi past, then the Simon Wiesenthal Center was the one most likely to be successful in such an endeavour.

Two weeks later they were utterly shocked at the letter they received from the American Wiesenthal Center. The experts there were in no doubt whatsoever. The photograph they had sent was of a senior Nazi officer called Heinz Christian Meyer who was assistant commandant of one of the most notorious SS concentration camps in Poland in which hundreds of thousands of Jews, gypsies and others had been murdered in the gas chambers. Even worse was the provenance of the list of names – it was a death list and all of those names with a tick beside them had been mercilessly slaughtered in the gas chambers as they all were indeed Jewish. Jane had correctly guessed their religion because of their surnames. Furthermore, they were all listed as having been murdered in this way in the computerised records of *Yad Vashem* the famous and highly respected World Holocaust Remembrance Center in Jerusalem, Israel. So the two youngsters finally had their answer. Their wonderful and much-loved and honoured grandfather, who was known to all his family, friends, acquaintances and UK government officers as Hermann Braski, was none other than the evil war criminal SS assistant commandant Hauptsturmfuhrer (an SS Captain) Heinz Christian Meyer who had been on the Wiesenthal Center's wanted list ever since the war ended. The man had realised that there would be terrible retribution for the evil Nazi perpetrators of the Holocaust. So, as a very intelligent and resourceful man, he had managed somehow to leave Germany and falsify his name, and had ended up in England pretending to be a political refugee from an evil government which was effectively a brutal dictatorship. His entire subsequent life had been a complete lie – he had even tried to change his facial appearance both with some clever cosmetic surgery and the careful growing of a beard to help hide his facial features. Had he been subjected to judgement at the Nuremberg trials, then, in all probability, he would have been executed, or, at the very least, given a very substantial jail sentence as a significant and evil war criminal. Perhaps his particular affinity with Jewish people in all walks of life in England might have reflected extreme guilt, or, more likely, it was probably a ruse to put people off any scent about his true identity that may have emerged.

The two youngsters then had some key decisions to make. First, should they inform everyone else in their family of their grandfather's true identity? They would need to think very carefully about that, especially as his widow was still very frail and vulnerable. Second, was Hermann Braski, or, more truthfully, Hauptsturmfuhrer Heinz Meyer, a man who had truly redeemed himself by a subsequent life very well lived and full of benevolence following his earlier hideous transgressions of human decency? They were in no doubt about this second issue. The answer was an emphatic 'No'. There are some crimes that are so terrible and evil that they can never be forgiven, however good and productive a person's subsequent life may have been. For such abominable individuals there can never be true redemption. No redemption whatsoever. Sometimes even the young can show a degree of wisdom well beyond their years.

SELECT

Dennis Mannering was an ordinary boy. He knew it, and that was what annoyed him most. He had sat the H.A.R. examination the previous week and found it difficult. He had also witnessed the result as it was displayed on the Institute's central screen that very morning, and had cringed with embarrassment and frustration at that awful sight.

MANNERING DPL... REGION G2X1A South... H.A.R. 122... .CLASS B

Class B! He had considered this allocation as ridiculous as it was unfair, though, as yet, he was not entirely convinced of the validity of his doubts. But as he stood in the large hall with over one hundred other nervous sixteen-year-olds, he was certain of one thing. He just could not endure the disgrace of his failure.

His musing was interrupted by a shrill note emitted by a loudspeaker located on the wall at the far end of the hall. When empty of people, the hall had a rather desolate, almost ghostly air, but when inhabited, as it was at that moment, the metal panelling of the walls, the perforated ceiling and the hollow-sounding floor seemed somehow to reflect the mood of the children: tense, nervous and inhibited. Add to this the half-quenched feeling of expectancy that invariably precedes the demanding tests of an individual's intellect, and you have an idea of the charged atmosphere which the clear authoritative voice momentarily punctured.

'Attention! Attention!'

One hundred-and-six young hearts pounded in their hosts' ribcages.

'This announcement concerns all students currently assembled in Central Hall Number One. The teaching machines are now ready for you.'

There was a long pause. Dennis's stomach gave forth such an intense rumble that his understandable embarrassment almost equalled his apprehension.

The voice continued. 'You have already received your Registration cards. You must now complete them by filling in the relevant data. It is of the utmost importance, both for your own and our sakes, that you do this with total accuracy. Those who have forgotten may wish to be reminded that…'

Dennis had already stopped listening. Besides, with not atypical foresight he had already completed his card and had carefully placed it inconspicuously in his shirt pocket to hide the information of which he was so ashamed. In reality, his mediocre credentials were all the more conspicuous for being concealed. When the announcement had ended, Dennis and the others were ushered out of the hall by several officials (who were, he thought, unusually courteous for educationalists), and directed along the giant corridors to the appropriate Education Rooms where the teaching machines were housed.

PERIOD 5

... Intellectually undesirable as it was, the advent of academic selectivity on the basis of H.A.R. attainment was nevertheless a socially predictable consequence of the widespread adoption of right-wing extremism and elitism. This unhealthy, though fortunately transient, phenomenon was evident mainly in Europe but also to a smaller extent in the USA. Africa and Asia had remained comparatively free. The development was well described by a notable British politician as having made the advocates of the triumph of enlightened reason over bigoted prejudice turn over in their graves.

Indeed, by all accounts, the distinguishing feature of the trend was an almost total disregard for the individual child. Only the exceptionally gifted or retarded were given any degree of special consideration. From a remarkably early age the children were compelled to compete in an academic jungle in which only those who managed to score highly in the H.A.R. tests stood any chance of proceeding to higher education in the universities. In short, the academic 'rat-race' was extended to an unprecedented degree.

... The fundamental fallacy implicit in this rigid educational system concerns the supposed validity which the educationalists attributed to the H.A.R., also known as the Hoffman Ability Rating. The accuracy of this test was tragically over-estimated, even by some of the most eminent authorities of the day.

... Yet this was only one instance of a more general social decay. The few who foresaw the abyss into which society was plunging were not powerful or vocal enough to do anything of an appreciable nature. Their pleas had also come too late. The social climate was firmly geared to short-sightedness, and society's long struggle to dispel and eliminate the more creative elements of its youth was clearly succeeding.

... The teaching machines, which had made such a promising beginning in the previous decade, aptly reflected society's failure to harness genuine originality from its youth.

After a journey which seemed intolerably long, Dennis eventually reached the east wing of the Institute which included in its confines the Education Rooms of which there were seven. These were referred to as Rooms A, B, C, D, E, G and M, corresponding to graduation in levels of 'ability' ranging from 'very good' – H.A.R: 130-150; 'good' – H.A.R: 120-130; 'average' – H.A.R: 100-120; 'below average' – H.A.R: 80-100; to 'poor' – H.A.R: 60-80.

That left G and M. The authorities thought naively that by refraining from publicly announcing the meanings of 'G' and 'M', they would avoid undue embarrassment. There were, however, few people who did not think that these initials stood for 'Geniuses' and 'Morons'.

Red-cheeked and sweating, Dennis stood perfunctorily outside the door of his classroom with about twenty other 'B-clubs' as they were euphemistically called by the officials. Inscribed in neat gold lettering on the upper half of the steel door was the following:

ROOM B 120-130

NO SMOKING

A short, stocky, middle-aged man with tiny cold grey eyes above an obtrusive hooked nose exuded a sickly smile.

'Right, boys and girls. Shall we go in?'

No reply was expected, and none given.

Once he had entered the room, Dennis found his anxiety dwindling. He had imagined the room to be a nightmare of electronic terrors. After all, he, like all of his friends, had heard the rumours of the photo-electric eyes that scrutinised one's every move, the electronic chair in which one was forced to sit for hours on end and, worst of all, the electrodes that were inserted into one's arms, legs, chest and head. However, his apparently irrational fears seemed to be groundless.

The room was extremely large, circular in shape, and adequately equipped with efficient air-conditioning. The teaching machines appeared to be rather smaller than he had imagined. There were thirty of them spaced at regular intervals around the room. The central area was unoccupied by machinery, and it was here that the two elderly supervisors sat pensively at their desks. It was their duty to co-ordinate the lessons with the different age groups and to deal with any difficulty that might arise in connection with the machines. But the authorities had gone to considerable lengths to ensure that the probability of such events occurring was extremely low. In fact, only two incidents of this kind had ever occurred officially, and these under very mysterious circumstances. Consequently, those at the top were understandably reluctant to talk about them to anyone, least of all to prospective students.

As soon as the train of youngsters had stepped into the room, the taller of the two supervisors gave a sharp twitch of his scraggy moustache and motioned the children to take seats beside the machines.

'You can sit anywhere you like. It makes no difference. The machines are identical.' After a brief pause, the supervisor went on. 'Now, first drop your blue cards into the slit provided on the working surface, and wait ten seconds. Then carefully put on the earphones provided, press the red button and wait. That's all you have to do. The machine takes over and gives you instructions after that. Most of them have a male voice but some female voices have been included for the sake of variation!'

A scarcely audible titter followed. Somewhat hurt by the poor response to his last remark, he concluded his introduction abruptly. 'Right then, it's all yours. The machines will tell you when to stop. They turn themselves off automatically.'

For a long while, Dennis stared blankly at the masterpiece of engineering that confronted him. It was coated with what appeared to be a dark green veneer of some artificial material, moulded in the shape of a square desk about five feet in height. The chair in which he sat was placed about a foot away from the machine and afforded easy access to the upper working surface of the desk. On the latter he found a large paper pad over which was suspended a small independent rectangular scanner. The desk also provided additional lighting for the convenience of the student. To the right of the pad were two rows of control buttons beside which he found a small, elongated recess containing various writing materials including several differently coloured pencils.

Impressed by its compactness as a whole, he explored the machine further, more hastily now since most of the others had already started. In the upper half of the vertical surface directly facing him Dennis noticed a number of dials and a small grille, the functions of which he had scarcely had time to consider. On the right side of the machine was attached a long plastic lever below which was a notice:

PULL ONLY IN CASE OF EXTREME EMERGENCY

Above this was a small circular panel with a lock situated centrally. The entire complex was surrounded by a transparent canopy which served as a soundproofing device. What he did not see were two long thin metal leads emerging from the bottom of the machine and connecting to a hidden socket in the wall, this in turn communicating with a central computer housed in an adjoining room.

Dennis dropped his card into the slit, donned the earphones, and pushed the button as instructed. For a short period of a few seconds he could hear a faint purring which slightly irritated both sides of his head. It was an odd feeling, yet not actually unpleasant. The purring stopped, and a clear yet distinctly metallic female voice (he was one of the 'lucky' ones) spoke to him.

'Good afternoon, Dennis'. (How did it know his first name the boy wondered? After all, his card only said MANNERING DPL).

'Good afternoon,' was his reflex reply.

'I am generally addressed as Philip.'

'Philip!' exclaimed Dennis, adjusting his earphones to ensure that some mechanical defect hadn't disturbed the incoming sound waves.

'Yes, that is correct,' came the reply. 'It stands for F.I.L.I.P. B.' (Philip spelt it out letter by letter.) 'Can you guess what the initials stand for?'

'Fellow of the Institute of Literary and Itinerant Prodigies?'

'No. Feedback Inhibited For Learning And Instructional Programming,' the machine continued. 'In fact, however anthropomorphic I may appear to you, I am basically just a highly complex and sophisticated conglomeration of electronic circuits, cells and memory tapes.'

'Aren't we all?' asked Dennis thoughtfully.

'No, not quite. You see Dennis,' (Philip's tone was just a little patronizing), 'apart from the more obvious structural and functional differences between your brain and mine, we differ in that whereas you are capable of programming yourself, I am not. My instructional memory bank has to be periodically adjusted. Now, when computerised teaching was in its early stages, scientists were unable to "humanise" their machines. They somewhat naively attempted to do so by employing classical feedback principles whereby a particular answer from the subject could be dealt with by any one of a <u>limited</u> number of responses, which in turn would either confirm or else help alter, if necessary, the original answer. But this method was far too crude.

'Insight behaviour on the part of the machines could only develop when the human nervous system and certain physiological processes were more fully understood. Once the breakthrough had been achieved, humans were in a position to construct the forerunners of machines as complex and sophisticated as myself.

'The essence of our functioning is that by monitoring and rapidly analysing the form of your brainwaves, heart rate, blood pressure etc., we are able to "optimally adapt" to your characteristic behaviour. To put it more simply, we adjust to your "wavelength of living". We do this by means of the earphones.'

At this, Dennis's heart rate leapt by at least twenty pulses.

'No, don't worry! You will never feel any discomfort whatsoever,' Philip reassured him. 'You see, it's not so much that I can organise new patterns of responses without any obvious stimulus or past experience, as you can, but more that I can predict what your responses and "feelings" will be, and then deal with them in the best possible way, and without ever losing my temper since I haven't really got one to lose. Are you happier now?'

'I think so,' was Dennis's reply. But predictably he had not fully understood all that the machine had told him. He wasn't meant to.

'So shall we start Dennis?'

'I'm ready when you are.'

'Good!'

There was a short pause.

'Now, you will probably find the question I am going to ask you rather unusual, and somewhat different from those you have been used to. All you need to do is relax, let your mind roam, and allow your thoughts to be as varied as possible.'

When Philip had stopped speaking, the outer part of what had appeared to be a grille suddenly slid upwards into the metal framework of the machine, revealing a small glass screen.

'I'm sorry if that startled you,' said Philip. 'Soon you will see three shapes appear on the screen. What you have to do is construct as many single shapes as possible using only the three shapes given. Use the writing pad in front of you. I can see everything you write. Take as much time as you need, and if you get stuck for ideas then I shall help you. Do you understand?'

The answer was in the affirmative. Within a few seconds the three geometrical shapes appeared on the screen.

Ten minutes and seventeen writing sheets later Dennis was exhausted of ideas. He had thought of no less than seventy-one different shapes, each an original conception in itself, differing perceptibly in spatial orientation from the one before. Variations of angular relationships had been fully explored, as had shade and colour; he had used different colours to add to the already startling diversity. Most interesting of all, the more obvious shapes had been left to the very end, as if they were afterthoughts.

Philip gave an appreciative purr. 'That's good.'

Dennis acknowledged the complimentary verdict. Both machine and boy knew that the performance was more than good. It was an outstanding example of divergent thinking. The exercise was repeated with different combinations. Then more complex shapes were given, and these were followed by whole words. In each case, Dennis had no difficulty in thinking up scores of ingenious variations and solutions. Finally, he was asked to give a list of all the uses a toilet roll could be put to. Within a few minutes he had thought of no less than twenty-three, including as a Christmas decoration, a hammock for tired guineapigs, a pencil holder and a means of mummifying people who ask such stupid questions!

When the hour was over, the 'lesson' was terminated. Dennis had clearly done exceptionally well. He wasn't meant to.

*

Dennis was unable to sleep that night since he was more in the mood for thinking. He thought about his great disappointment in failing to qualify for Class A, the disgrace he felt when informing his parents of the result, and the soothing words of his mother: 'Never mind dear, we still love you.'

His father had been equally kind and supportive, but was rather more sceptical of the result. Not accepting that his wish was probably father to the thought, as it were, he remarked that the 'failure' was probably due to the inaccuracy of those 'damned stupid' marking machines. After all, they weren't infallible were they?

Dennis also thought of Philip, his new benevolent teacher, the paragon of knowledge and efficiency. Admittedly, he had been just a little irritated by the machine's rather authoritative, almost arrogant, air, and the well-nigh impeccable English that it spoke, but all the same he felt a curious fondness for it, almost as if the machine was a human friend. Moreover, his great success in the mental exercises had boosted his confidence considerably, and had reinforced his opinion that he was truly 'Class A material'. He realised well enough that, being his first lesson, the machine was very likely to allow him to do well to maintain his morale, but he felt that Philip was just too surprised at the sheer magnitude of his success. Although, officially, a student could only be promoted to a higher class after at least one year, Dennis was determined to prove his ability to the educationalists much sooner than that. It would be difficult for sure, but somehow, he would find a way.

*

The following weeks brought little change in Dennis's performance in the Education Room. If anything, the standard he had shown on that first day had been slightly surpassed. It was only with the more conventional type of work, most notably in mathematics and physics, that he found any degree of difficulty. Being well-read (unlike many of the Class A students), he shone in literature and philosophy, and possessing a natural linguistic talent (which ran in the family and was due, so his father said, to their rabbinical ancestry), he toyed with French, German, Russian and Esperanto. Meanwhile, a close relationship (if that is possible) developed between Philip and Dennis, for 'Phil', as the boy affectionately called the machine, had helped him enormously in his studies, and he was grateful for it.

Only once had they exchanged harsh words. They had just finished a particularly successful session in which Dennis had demonstrated his prowess in translating French verse into German prose. Feeling more proud of himself than ever, he had casually remarked that he was obviously good enough for Class A or maybe even Class G! The machine instantly sprang to the attack.

'You should not say that,' it told him.

'Why not?' asked Dennis. 'I don't see what's wrong…'

'You must not even think about it.'

'But please tell me why not Phil.'

'Aren't you happy as you are in Class B with me?' Philip's tone was almost pleading.

'Well, yes of course I am, but…'

'Then why do you wish to change?'

Dennis could feel his temper rising. 'I didn't say I <u>wanted</u> to change… Look, I was just pleased with how I'd done.'

Philip appeared to give way. 'Alright. I am sorry if I upset you. It is just that I am programmed to consider your general welfare as well as your education, and I would not like you to be hurt in any way.'

Dennis composed himself. 'OK, let's just drop the subject.'

The lesson ended as it had begun – in silence.

The episode was never mentioned again by either machine or boy. But it had made Dennis's strong desire to test himself with a Class A machine almost unbearably intense. A week later an opportunity to do this arose.

A currently famous and much lauded politician had been invited by the Institute to deliver a lecture entitled 'The importance of specialisation in contemporary education', and all students, with the notable exception of the 'M-clubs', were required to attend. The occasion was considered to be so important that even the supervisors, caretakers and other anonymous officials were expected to make an appearance. Consequently, the Education Rooms were likely to be relatively deserted and probably unguarded. The temptation, naturally, was too great for Dennis to resist, and he decided to go ahead with the plan he had been secretly contriving for weeks.

*

The cloying smell of the artificial leather corridor walls with their endless array of neat metal studs reminded Dennis of his early childhood, though he was not quite sure why. This uniformity typified everything that he experienced in a world where anything which failed to comply with the general scheme of clockwork living was considered to be useless. Thus MANNERING DPL, one of a new breed of young dissenters, was useless. Awkward, unintelligent in some areas perhaps, maybe creative, but regarded as useless all the same.

But he was still mature enough to realise that it was not worth brooding over a bad lot any longer. However dubious the results of the H.A.R. tests may have been, he <u>had</u> after all given a mediocre performance, and it was up to him to use what ability he had to get promotion. Yet, unusually self-critical for one so young, he was reluctant to identify exactly why he wanted to be promoted. It was strange, he reflected, that people seldom find rational explanations for their most highly motivated behaviour. Perhaps one can only act completely logically when nothing critical is at stake. That was probably why he had done so badly in the tests. By desiring to excel more than anything else he had unwittingly put his thinking capacity in jeopardy. His more successful peers, who couldn't care less how well they performed in tests, did well precisely because their minds were uncluttered with worries and anxieties. He shuddered at this thought. If that were really the case, then he would almost certainly do badly with a Class A machine since he was so intent on doing well. If he could just make himself relax, even for a short time, then he should have a good chance of succeeding.

It was never wise to daydream anywhere within the Education Institute. For quite apart from the obvious physical danger it involved of injuring oneself by colliding with a burly caretaker or, even worse, falling down one of the numerous escalators, he also ran the risk of being spotted by an official (or a vicious fellow student) and being reported to the welfare authorities as psychologically unbalanced. But realising the risk he was running, he took appropriate action: he opened his eyes wide, assumed an uncharacteristically alert expression and began to walk as briskly and purposefully as his nervous legs would allow.

It was just as well that he did this, since a group of seven A-clubs had just emerged from a nearby lift, and was approaching him at an uncomfortably rapid rate. In his mind, Dennis had divided A-clubs into two distinct groups. There were the quiet, academic kind who, like himself, were intelligent, tolerant, broad minded and liberal. Then there were the bigoted breed who, although it has to be admitted were adept at passing difficult examinations, were far more conscious of their social and intellectual status than their more modest fellows. These 'undesirables' tended, in general, to be aggressive towards those they considered their social and mental inferiors, and were therefore regarded by the other students with a combination of contempt and fear. As might be expected, they were also the type who were more likely to inform the authorities of any behavioural defect of the more sensitive students, including their fellow A-clubs. It just so happened that those who were walking towards Dennis were members of this unattractive group.

Dennis knew that they were A-clubs mainly because he had seen several of them ushered away by A-club officials on Registration Day (How long ago that seemed!), and A-clubs seldom socialised with anyone outside their own class. When they were within about ten yards he deduced that they were undesirables, partly because of the uniformly supercilious expressions on their faces. His major worry was that one or more of them would report him as deliberately cutting the lecture. It was obvious that he was doing so since he was heading in the opposite direction to the General Lecture Hall. How would he explain his behaviour to the authorities? He had told no-one of his intentions, not even his parents or Philip B, and would have nobody to confirm any of the alibis he might be forced to concoct. There was also the unlikely possibility that the advancing A-clubs would try to physically prevent him from entering forbidden territory.

Just as the group was passing him, one of them, a tall lean young man with closely cropped hair and a face with strong Roman features, gave Dennis a rather surprised yet decidedly vicious glance. He nudged one of the others sharply; they looked towards Dennis and, apparently indifferent to his presence, passed him without any comment or action. The troublemaker seemed mildly disappointed at his comrades' lack of interest, but knew not to push them too far. Never mind, there would be other opportunities in the future to have some fun with these losers.

There was not far to go, just two escalators and then only a narrow gallery would separate him from the realm of talent. Although he was exceptionally nervous, he was completely convinced that he was doing the right thing. The educational system as it stood was both unjust and ineffective so it was necessary to expose its faults for all to see. It had never occurred to him that an unjust society seldom admits its mistakes willingly. Almost by definition, its cruel iniquity guarantees the almost impossibly difficult measures needed by a just minority to secure its overthrow. He was not only afraid of losing face in front of his own intellect (however paradoxical that may seem), or of letting down society. He was also unsure of the warning Philip B had given him during that argument that he had tried so hard to forget: 'I would not like you to be hurt in any way.' Presumably, 'hurt' referred to a psychological wound, which might result from a failure to qualify at the higher level. But what if it didn't? Suppose the penalty for even trying to stray out of one's own class was a physical punishment, akin to the ritual school canings of antiquity? Or perhaps he might be physically liquidated. This was unthinkable. Yet not so long before, it had been unthinkable to imagine himself as anything other than an A-club. The trouble with the 'unthinkable' was that it was invariably the most likely thing to happen.

As Dennis hurried through the glass-roofed gallery, his face was showered with the gentle warmth of a beautiful June morning. This was one of the few areas within the Institute where the sun's golden rays could really penetrate. It seemed at first to put everything that was happening into perspective. It also added a touch of bravado to the situation. For a moment, Dennis saw himself as a bold explorer of space, braving the dangers of a hostile alien environment with scornful indifference, completely aware of the uncertainty of his movements yet enjoying to the utmost the challenge of the unknown and the status he knew would be accorded to his select profession.

ROOM A 130-150
STUDENTS ARE REQUESTED TO REFRAIN FROM SMOKING

At least, Dennis thought, that was one rule which seemed to apply to all classes. It was remarkable that almost a hundred years after a direct causal relationship had been demonstrated conclusively between smoking and lung cancer, as well as other cancers and diseases, about one-fifth of the population worldwide were still unable to forego this dubious pleasure. With a little luck, there would be a fair smattering of educationalists among them.

If anyone of any importance happened to be passing the entrance to Room A, and had seen Dennis in the process of summoning the courage to open the door and enter, he would have been in very serious trouble. He knew this well enough, but in view of the mass exodus to the General Lecture Theatre, he had considered the risk worth running. Imagine his surprise, then, when he noticed that the key to the room had been left in the door. What sort of an institution was it, he wondered, that lay down some of the strictest rules ever known in a school of learning, yet through its own negligence, virtually encouraged its subjects to break them? If they had given him a B for ability then he would reciprocate by awarding them a C minus for consistency.

He turned the key, depressed the cold metal handle, and slowly pushed the large steel door open. He then entered the room on tiptoe and quietly closed the door behind him. As far as he could see, the room was empty, with not a supervisor in sight. It was almost a complete replica of Room B (and, he presumed, of Rooms C, D, E and F. Rooms G and M were complete mysteries). The only differences were minor: there were rather more windows in the higher regions of the walls above the teaching machines, the floor was covered by an attractive blue mottled carpet instead of the grey linoleum of Room B, and the room was slightly smaller. The teaching machines themselves were coloured light blue rather than dull green, and this helped to give the room a much brighter and livelier ambience.

Feeling that time was precious, he took a seat beside the nearest machine. The controls were identical to those of Philip B. He inserted his card into the slit and carefully placed the earphones onto his head. Then he hesitated. Surely, he thought, the machine would immediately recognise him as a fraud. But, he reasoned, it wouldn't actually matter as long as he could prove his high intelligence. Then the machine would have a permanent record of what he had done. Whatever else they might be, the educationalists weren't complete fools however misguided they might be. They were bound to be impressed with his brain power and enterprise. Then they would see what talent they were missing. So he pressed the red button.

Almost immediately he could hear the familiar purr through the earphones. But it was a louder, more intense noise than he was used to, and the machine spoke to him clearly in a male voice, more clipped and powerful than that of Philip B.

'Good morning, Dennis.' (Again, it knew his first name.)

'Good morning Philip.' He could not prevent his voice from shaking.

'How are you feeling today?'

'Fine, thank you. I am a little frustrated though... And how are you?'

'Fully functional Dennis. I can only assume that you feel frustrated because you consider yourself to have been unfairly placed in a class whose academic standard does little justice to your exceptional ability.'

This was surprisingly direct. It made Dennis tread more warily than he had intended. 'I wouldn't go that far, Philip. Let's just say that I think I should be given another chance to prove that I am Class A material.'

'You don't consider yourself exceptional?' There was genuine surprise in the machine's artificial voice.

'Not really. Exceptional is a word that should always be used with some reservation. Unless you mean that I have exceptionally bad luck in which case I am certainly exceptional.'

The machine's tone softened. 'Yes indeed. Tell me Dennis, what do you want me to do for you?'

'Haven't I made that clear already?'

'You wish to be tested?'

'Yes I do.'

'Now?'

'Yes, if it's convenient for you. As you obviously know I am here under rather dubious circumstances.'

'So you came to this room in the full knowledge that it is strictly forbidden to do so.'

'Yes, but…'

'Never mind Dennis, no harm has been done, at least not yet.'

There was a pause for about fifteen seconds before the machine continued. 'Should you fail, then I shall inform no-one that you were here.'

'Thank you, Philip. Much appreciated.' He was beginning to relax.

'Well, we may as well start. If you are really as good as you seem to think, then I shall advise the authorities to seriously consider your somewhat eccentric application for promotion. Right, let's start with something easy,' the machine continued. 'Define psychology as briefly as you can.'

Dennis thought for a few seconds then said, 'Psychology is the study of perception.'

'That's very good,' said Philip A. 'Here's a harder one for you. Define philosophy, in rather more detail this time.'

Dennis had a major interest in Philosophy and he was ready for this one so there was no delay. 'Philosophy is an analysis of thought and matter reconciled with human experience, and is therefore directed towards the acquisition, realisation and rationalisation of all human experience and knowledge, no matter whence it comes.'

'That's excellent. But I do think testing can be a very inexact business, don't you?'

'Oh yes,' Dennis replied. 'The examiners can make so many mistakes in marking the papers.'

'Quite. Incidentally, do you know Gregorio's principle of historical ideas?'

'Yes, I've just been reading one of his books called "The Realist's Approach to History". I think his main thesis is that people who change and enlighten society seldom put forward wholly original ideas. Their greatness can lie more in their ability to place the right emphasis on the relevant ideas of the past.'

Philip A purred softly. 'That's it exactly. In fact, as you may know, Gregorio's great uncle…'

'Luigi Gregorio?'

'Right again, Dennis. Old Luigi, of course, was quite a brain, probably the most creative of the philosophers living in the second half of the last century. What is the basic postulate of what he called "thought-frame introspection"?'

Dennis needed a little time for this. 'Old Luigi' tended to be rather verbose, and it was notoriously difficult to quote him accurately. But he managed to do it all the same. 'Yes, he said that… er, each… er, … each single idea which allows a free association of thoughts can be called a "thought frame", for it is as if the idea is the only restraining force available; it encompasses in the mental frame the thoughts which it evokes. The idea and frame can stimulate and hold together any number of thoughts. Yet it is really impossible to decide where one thought frame ends and a new one begins. For any one of the thoughts of a frame can itself constitute a new frame. Thus the idea of a frame is solely one of convenience as its boundaries are totally arbitrary.'

'Yes Dennis.' There was a brief yet somehow uncomfortable silence before the machine continued. 'Do you know that you are the third person from

Class B who has come to me hoping for promotion?'

'I shouldn't think I'll be the last either,' Dennis added airily.

'You are probably correct. There will certainly be others.' Philip A made a noise that sounded very much like a human sigh. Then, without any warning whatsoever, the machine attacked. 'Distinguish between socialism and communism.'

Dennis was caught unaware. 'I'm sorry, could you please repeat the question?'

'Distinguish between socialism and communism. A concise answer is required.'

'Well it depends on which…'

'So you don't know. How disappointing.'

'Just give me a moment to…'

'No I will not. Let's try something else. You say you like philosophy.'

'Yes I do but…'

'Distinguish between Kant's hypothetical and categorical imperatives.'

Dennis knew the answer but needed a little time to express himself. So he hesitated.

'Very well then. Distinguish between non-categorical and hypothetical propositions.'

'But I really haven't studied…'

'Surely you are acquainted with the basic principles of elementary logic?'

'But formal logic just isn't that important at my level.'

The machine seemed to be what humans would call angry – or at least irritated. 'Not true!' Philip asserted violently. 'Logic is the bedrock of thought. To study and understand it is one of the highest forms of human intellectual activity.'

'It's certainly one of them,' said Dennis.

'It is a supremely important aspect of philosophy and you clearly know virtually nothing about it. How disappointing you are. What are the fundamental principles of logical positivism and the theory of descriptions? To what extent are these related?'

'I think I need just a little time to answer that.'

'Alright. Distinguish between induction and deduction. Which of these is more important in scientific discovery?'

'Well, in one case…'

'Too slow. I want quicker answers. You are too hesitant and probably unsure of your ground. Explain Kant's notion that synthetic propositions can also be *a priori*. Give typical examples of such statements.'

'Well what I think he was getting at…'

'What you think? What you think?' Philip was now

very angry by any human standards. The machine was relentless and hardly allowed Dennis even to attempt the answers. 'What is the relationship between pure mathematics and formal logic?'

The voice of the machine and the normally faint background hum of the mains had become so loud as to be almost deafening. 'How many prime numbers are there between one and a hundred?'

Dennis had no answer, and began to plead. 'Stop the noise! Stop the noise please!' But he was unable to remove the earphones which seemed to be firmly attached to his head.

'Distinguish between hypothetical and disjunctive syllogisms!'

'You know I can't!'

Dennis became desperate and began to scream in short sharp bursts.

But the machine's brutal questioning was relentless. Dennis responded by uttering a continuous long drawn-out wail.

There was still the emergency lever!

With one superhuman effort, he extended his right arm and slowly groped towards the lever.

Philip appeared to become hysterical.

'Machines and men!'

But it was no use. The lever was just too far away.

'Teachers and pupils!'

Finally, Philip A shouted, 'Clever little boys and stupid little boys!'

At this, Dennis managed to concentrate for a few seconds. The words echoed in his mind bitterly.

'Clever little boys and stupid little boys!'

In a final qualm of nausea, and overpowered by the insurmountable pain which permeated his body and extended to the farthest reaches of his consciousness, Dennis retched and collapsed in a crumpled heap on the floor. Philip A had by now stopped the 'test' and purred contemptuously. A horizontal flash of light appeared for a few seconds on the screen at the front of the machine before a single word materialised and was visible to all.

MORON

THE LIGHT

It was dusk, and Incram surveyed the undulating rhythm of the valley spread out like a carpet before him. Despite his fifty years of existence on the planet, the sight of a desolate landscape shimmering beneath naked moonlight still filled him with a strange combination of awe and intense fear. He feared that the farthest extremities of the land might suddenly rise up like a tidal wave and completely engulf him, forming a mighty high-walled blanket that would surround struggling humanity, constricting and strangling it until it sank helplessly into the inner recesses of a cold dark earth. But tonight his fears were less than usual.

The Coming was near. He knew it, and he could feel it in his bones. True enough, there were a few members of his tribe who did not accept the prophecies of the Okadzi, and who scoffed at the Coming of The Light, dismissing it as giving a false hope. But he had lived longer than they, and had seen more of the wonders of the world and the secrets it revealed to true believers.

A few years before his untimely death, Incram's

father had told him that at some time in the future, foretold indirectly yet accurately by the Okadzi, The Light would come as it had once done during his lifetime. The Light would both provide salvation for all mankind and become an example for future progress. It would provide at one and the same time all the material needs of an inhabited world and the moral guidance, supreme edification and conscious purpose with which they could build a perfect society.

The last Light had failed, and for the sixty years since then, Incram's people had degenerated from a constructive to an almost pointless existence. But that last time the believers had been too few. They had, so his father had recounted, insulted the Spirit of Okadzi by not honouring its presence in a proper manner. The simpletons had tried to match the New Light's brilliance with an inferior light of their own which was not clear and godlike, but the dense and destructive light of a fire. The Light had taken revenge by destroying itself, and by doing so it had robbed the people of their ultimate salvation. But it would be different this time, for they were wiser now.

Incram reached into the breast pocket of his old leather jerkin, removed a small slim clothbound book, lifted his dark brown eyes towards the heavens above him and began to recite from memory.

'When three score years have passed since The Lesser Light, then shall The New Light be bestowed upon the face of the Earth. This New Light being more wonderful and possessed of far greater power than the one before, its subjects shall honour its presence as is best fitting. The Okadzi has willed it so.'

After a period of intense silence Incram put away the book, picked up the rest of his belongings which were strewn across the dense undergrowth around him, and started to walk in the direction of the lowlands. He had travelled over twenty miles since daylight had first appeared, and still had another three miles to cover before re-joining his tribe.

The Coming was near.

*

Most of the tribe were sleeping when Incram returned. The Coming would be at least four hours away, and they thought it wise to rest and conserve their energy. Only a handful of young children were awake, and they were whispering among themselves, huddled cosily together by the side of a small smouldering log-fire under the heavy evening darkness. When they saw Incram approaching, the whispering became louder, and many of the people were roused from sleep. One of these, a dishevelled elder called Ernwell, gently embraced Incram and asked him 'Is it tonight that The Light will come upon us?'

Incram smiled and answered, 'I believe it is.'

A throng had now formed a circle around Incram,

and stirred nervously at his words.

'There is no cause for alarm. We have only ourselves to fear. Remember the last Light and how shamefully our forefathers earned its disdain.'

'We shall not insult the Okadzi again,' replied Ernwell, 'but there have been strange omens in the skies for nearly a day now, tiny beacons that pulsate in rhythm with our fear. We do not understand them. Does it auger well for The Coming?'

Incram had seen them too and had been equally alarmed, though his father had told him that before The Light itself returned, the beacons would come. But, like all good leaders, he concealed his fear.

At this point, he decided to inspire his tribe. 'The fiery beacons herald the coming of The New Light. They are a wonder to behold! For years we have lived in squalor in this wilderness, existing on the pathetic offerings of nature. Our children are half-starved, inadequately clothed, and all of us are diseased, either in mind or body. Brothers and sisters – we have been slaves of our miserable surroundings, the underclass which is trampled on by our sadistic masters. We are about to fulfil our destiny!'

The throng was in raptures.

'The beacons are a signal for us to make due preparation for The Coming.'

The gathered mass of people lapsed into excited chatter. Incram cast a long wistful glance at the myriad stars above him. He was about to continue his speech when a bearded youth who had been hiding behind a nearby tree suddenly confronted him.

'Incram,' he cried, 'you are a blind fool! The beacons are warnings, not signals, warnings that we must stay well away from The Light.'

'Thenar,' replied Incram solemnly, 'you are entirely wrong, believe me. The Light is good. It is our saviour. It is…'

'The Light is evil!' screamed Thenar. 'It reeks of corruption. It is of no use at all to us.'

Predictably, the crowd did not take kindly to this blasphemous interjection.

'Foolish upstart!' someone yelled.

'Fools!' he screamed back.

But he had gone too far. At Incram's command, the young man was silenced, as gently as the laws of the Okadzi allowed.

'Come,' said Incram in a commanding tone after the fuss had died down, 'we must prepare.'

*

It came less than four hours later. Only 'It' was not one, but three separate Lights. Incram and his tribe gazed in awe at the Messengers of Okadzi as they fell silently through the zenith above them. It was some five minutes before anyone was able to see the Lights in any detail.

The most striking characteristic was their intense brilliance which made it almost impossible to look at them directly. At first, they appeared to slowly rotate around both their own and a common central axis. But after a dozen or so revolutions, their movements became much faster and more random. As soon as Incram thought he recognised a particular pattern thus formed by The Lights, then sure enough that apparent pattern would change gracefully into another. The Lights, radiant against the sombre darkness of the overlying heavens, sparkled and grew in intensity as the distance between them and the people gradually lessened.

Overcome by what she was witnessing, a young woman behind Incram closed her eyes, knelt down beside him and began to utter a familiar chant:

Light of the soul
Save us! Save us!
Love's fair halo
Guard us! Guard us!

Soon, the detailed outlines of The Lights became

visible to the earthbound. They seemed to be identical, although Incram could only see one of them particularly well. This was composed of two main interconnecting regions. One of these, the lower half, comprised the greater proportion of The Light. As far as he could see, this – The Light Proper – was basically rectangular in shape, and it was covered on its outer surface by a number of wide bands whose lateral borders were lined by a bluish tinge. Above, attached to and radiating out from The Light Proper by what appeared to be numerous silver filaments, Incram could just about discern the illuminated outline of a white disc.

By this time, almost all of the women and children, as well as a fair proportion of the men, had joined in the rhythmic doggerel, which became louder in time with the increasing brightness of the descending Lights. To get a clearer view of the disc, Incram joined some of his fellows who had positioned themselves half-way up a nearby hillock. From this vantage point he noticed that the disc was distinctly concave in shape, thus giving it the appearance of a halo.

Halo of the Light
Guard and protect us
Love us! Love us!
Give us what we crave!

It had been done. The Light would soon reach the tribe, and all were ready to accept its bidding – even Thenar. Incram looked down into the glade that was his home, and the isolated clusters of humanity that eagerly awaited the chance of a new life in the shelter of The Light. He had no greater conception of what The Lights contained than they. But his lips grew into a beatific smile. The New Light had come.

SPIDER

'Can you see it yet?' asked the fair-haired boy of his younger friend.

'No I can't. It's impossible,' John replied as he squinted his right eye in the hope that this might make it work. The pupil was already very small.

'Perhaps if you bring the torch a bit nearer it might work.'

The narrow beam from the pocket torch was brought to within a few centimetres of the child's right eye. The eyelids opened and closed rhythmically in response to the regular vertical motion of the torch. The entire length of John's body was tensed in expectation of the visual wonder that had been promised him. Then, and without any warning whatsoever, it came, as quick as the flash that had produced it.

'Roger, I can see it! It's there!' His face contorted strangely from a mingled sense of wonder and fear as he said, 'Look for yourself!' to his friend.

'How can I see it idiot? Come on, tell me – what exactly can you see?'

'Well, it's sort of creepy and horrible… sort of like a spider's web or jagged rocks on a mountain, and they all come from a hole in the middle, and…'

'What shape is it exactly and what colour?'

John frowned. 'It's mainly round like a circle and kind of browny-red, but the lines are also black just like a spider's legs.'

'All spindly and horrible?'

'Yes, all spindly and horrible.' John's lips began to quiver nervously. 'Roger, I'm scared.'

Roger smiled. 'I was first time too, but you soon get over it.'

'I don't want to see it anymore. Can you stop it? I'm getting a headache.'

'But you might never get it again,' Roger replied. 'You know, you're very lucky because you got it first go. It took me ages to see it like you have.'

'But it's going already. Are you still moving the torch? It's now gone all silvery and it's got holes in it… Hey, I can now see your face through it.'

'Fool! I told you it would fade away if you didn't keep concentrating. Now keep it there!'

Roger waved the torch furiously, and his younger friend tried his best to hold the image.

'It's coming back! I can see the creepy lines again.'

'What else can you see?'

'The legs are sort of deep, right into the circle and dancing with themselves and laughing all because I can't touch them.'

'What else?'

'Oh it's much clearer now. But it's worse. The spider's coming towards me, it's going to eat my eyes out and tickle my brains. It's spitting hot red stuff all over my eyelashes... Please Roger... stop it!'

'What else do you see? Tell me!'

'It's all wriggling and getting bigger and smaller like someone breathing and like a spider who's going to crush and squeeze and eat its victim.' The boy put his hands around his slender throat. 'Roger?'

'Yes?'

'I think I'm going to be sick.'

'Not over me you're not.'

'Please Roger.'

His gaze and will softened. 'OK, I'll stop it for a bit.'

'Thank you.'

*

The remarkably obese doctor closed the bedroom door and spoke quietly. 'It's only a small stye. It shouldn't take more than a few days to clear up. Anyway, this ointment should help the discomfort a little.'

John's mother was not entirely convinced. 'He says it hurts him terribly.'

'They usually sting a little. I shouldn't worry.'

'But the right eye is so red.'

'Mrs Davies, I've said it's nothing to worry about.'

'I've seen what can happen when it gets bad.'

'Bad? What do you mean?' the doctor asked her.

'The eye itself. It can swell until it might burst.'

'Nonsense. The only issues are social ones.'

'But aren't they bad enough?'

'No, of course not. I suppose it really depends on the person and those with whom one socialises. Anyway, as I told you, this really is nothing at all serious.'

'He keeps complaining of "spiders" in his eye.'

'I know. John told me. What an imagination your son has!' The doctor pouted his thick lips and nodded slowly. 'That's a good sign.'

*

The bedroom air settled lazily on the filtered sunlight emerging from the bay window, and then spread widely throughout the room to produce a sense of mild oppressiveness. The boy raised himself from summer's gentle slumber and felt his right eye. Since morning it had steadily increased in size in response to the spider's pressure and was approaching the limits of the eye's natural elasticity.

A pocket-torch lay on the wooden cabinet beside the bed, and beneath this was a small penknife with a razor-sharp blade resting in anticipation. Slowly and carefully John lifted the torch and shone it rhythmically into the side of his right eye. It didn't take long to appear. The spider's legs and jagged body were there again as usual, as if laughing and insulting him. He lifted the knife and took careful aim.

ABOUT THE AUTHOR

Peter GE Kennedy CBE, MD, PhD, DSc, is a distinguished clinician and scientist who held the Burton Chair of Neurology for 29 years (1987-2016) at Glasgow University where he remains active in research and teaching as a Professor and Honorary Senior Research Fellow in the Institute of Neuroscience and Psychology. He also has two master's degrees in philosophy, has written nine previous novels, a book of poetry, an award-winning popular science book on African Sleeping Sickness, and co-edited two textbooks on neurological infections. He has received numerous awards for his research work, most recently the Royal Medal of the Royal Society of Edinburgh (RSE). He is a fellow of both the Academy of Medical Sciences and the RSE.

BY THE SAME AUTHOR
ALSO AVAILABLE ON AMAZON:

TIMELESS MEMORIES (2022)
PROFESSIONAL MADNESS (2021)
TWO CENTURIES OF DOUBT (2021)
THE IMAGE IN MY MIND (2020)
ARCADIAN MEMORIES AND OTHER POEMS (2020)
THE FATAL SLEEP (2019) - Luath Press, 3rd Edition
TWELVE MONTHS OF FREEDOM (2019)
CATAPULT IN TIME (2018)
RETURN OF THE CIRCLE (2017)
BROTHERS IN RETRIBUTION (2015)
REVERSAL OF DAVID (2014)

Printed in Great Britain
by Amazon